"THE TARGET MUST BE DESTROYED!"

Major Normand watched the fighter escort as they dipped their wings in salute and headed home.

"Enemy fighters! Eight o'clock, high!"

His mind was jarred roughly back to reality. Singly and in groups of three, four, and five, the fighters came at them. All types of fighters struck viciously at the formation.

The 305th staggered through the holocaust, and Normand's hands trembled as one by one B-17's of the group broke apart and headed earthward.

"Let's make a separate run," the bombardier called.

"Stay with the formation!" Normand said quickly. He knew something the bombardier did not—there were only two other planes left in the 305th!

*Other War Books
from Jove*

**AIR WAR SOUTH ATLANTIC
BATAAN: THE MARCH OF DEATH
GUADALCANAL
HITLER MUST DIE
THE KAMIKAZES
NIGHT DROP: THE AMERICAN
AIRBORNE INVASION OF NORMANDY
PATTON'S BEST**

THE INCREDIBLE 305ᵀᴴ
The "Can Do" Bombers of World War II

WILBUR H. MORRISON

A JOVE BOOK

This Jove book contains the complete
text of the original hardcover edition.
It has been completely reset in a typeface
designed for easy reading and was printed
from new film.

THE INCREDIBLE 305th

A Jove Book / published by arrangement with
E. P. Dutton, Inc.

PRINTING HISTORY
Duell, Sloan & Pearce edition published 1962
Jove edition / August 1984
Second printing / March 1987

All rights reserved.
Copyright © 1962 by Wilbur H. Morrison.
This book may not be reproduced in whole or in part,
by mimeograph or any other means, without permission.
For information address: E. P. Dutton, Inc.,
2 Park Avenue, New York, NY 10016.

ISBN: 0-515-09027-1

Jove Books are published by The Berkley Publishing Group,
200 Madison Avenue, New York, NY 10016.
The words "A JOVE BOOK" and the "J" with sunburst
are trademarks belonging to Jove Publications, Inc.

PRINTED IN THE UNITED STATES OF AMERICA

to
RALPH McKEE
and
BOB WIRT

ACKNOWLEDGMENTS

A fighting organization has little time for paper work, and the 305th was no exception. The exploits described in this book represent only a fraction of the deeds of the men, living and dead, who dedicated themselves to the preservation of freedom.

The author would like to express his appreciation to the following at the United States Air Force Historical Division, Montgomery, Alabama, for their patience and perseverance in uncovering the details of the group's history: Dr. Albert F. Simpson, Chief of the Division, Marguerite K. Kennedy, Chief of the Archives, and archivists Clark Palmer, Ruth Gaines, and Frank Myers.

In particular, the author owes a special debt of gratitude to Colonel Frank L. O'Brien, Lieutenant Colonel Ralph D. McKee, Major Robert E. Wirt, Major James F. Sunderman, and Airman First Class Wilbur A. Julian.

CONTENTS

    Prologue   1

1 "Boomtown's" Incredible Flight   7
    ... the Fortress staggered away from the blistering attack.

2 The Cabin Seemed to Explode   21
    ... the copilot saw with horror that Taylor had been killed instantly.

3 "Bail Out! Bail Out!"   33
    ... the plane was uncontrollable.

4 A Magnificent Team   47
    ... "today's mission to Vegesack is unmatched in the annals of the air war in Europe to date."

5	A Day to Remember	57
	...the ferocity of the attacks was indicated by the claims.	
6	"I'll Fly Tail-End Charlie Too!"	71
	...the indomitable spirit of a fighting Irishman.	
7	A Trail of Burning Fortresses	79
	...B-17's were going down in such numbers that he lost count.	
8	"The Target Must Be Destroyed!"	91
	..."today's operation is the most important yet conducted in this war."	
9	Distinguished Unit Citation	105
	...accomplishment of the assigned task was due to their extraordinary heroism.	
10	A Nightmarish Encounter with Death	113
	...the United States paid its greatest tribute.	
11	Berlin!	121
	...they knew Goering's boys would dispute every foot of the way.	
12	The Nation's Highest Award	131
	...the brave pilot's blood formed in pools on the floor of the plane.	

13 D-DAY   139
      ..."if you see fighting aircraft over
      you, they will be ours."

14 GROUP COMMANDER LOST IN ACTION   149
      ...the aircraft went into a flat spin and
      struck the ground with a flaming
      impact.

15 THE UNDERGROUND   159
      ...they risked death to rescue the fliers.

16 WAR OF ATTRITION   169
      ...both the Allies and the Germans
      probed continuously for weak spots in
      the others' defenses.

17 MASSIVE AERIAL ASSAULT   175
      ...it was the most merciless and
      gigantic air offensive in the history of
      warfare.

18 SYMBOL OF TRIUMPH   185
      ...it was a fitting climax in recognition
      of the group's efforts.

    EPILOGUE   193

PROLOGUE

Long before airmen of the United States Army Air Forces arrived in England during World War II to test a new concept of precision bombing with the Norden bombsight, the British Royal Air Force had fought the Luftwaffe to a standstill in the Battle of Britain and had entered on a night campaign of massive retaliation.

The British had developed bombers which could carry heavy loads of all kinds of bombs. Without an accurate bombsight, the R.A.F. made extensive use of the "saturation" method.

The Germans had early-warning radar, but the British had fighter direction radar and the highly effective "Gee." With this system, radar signals were transmitted from England to assist a bomber navigator in determining his position in the air in relation to the location of the target. If the signals were satisfactorily interpreted, the navigator could set up a bomb release point that, theoretically, was accurate to a tenth of a mile. Using this capability, the R.A.F. sent their bombers over the Channel carefully spaced as to altitude, lateral position, and time of passage. The bombers were so dispersed they appeared on the German radars like a bit of the firmament moving at a different speed. The problems of interception were enormous, and British losses were kept at a low level.

The British fought courageously, but their "saturation" techniques left much to be desired in the way of bombing accuracy. Large areas were bombed just to assure that selected military targets were hit.

American planners, who had announced their belief in the greater effectiveness of daylight bombing, had no illusions that the defensive power of the B-17 Flying Fortress was adequate to protect individual aircraft on daylight operations. Mass formations were planned by the AAF from the start, long before sufficient quantities of the heavy bombers were available.

The Eighth Air Force, having announced beforehand its faith in the accuracy of daylight operations, had a tiger by the tail. The proponents of this form of strategic bombing soon were called upon to prove their theories.

The story of how the early groups faced the challenge, and why they fought with such incredible devotion, has long intrigued me. After I became interested in writing a book, I visited the United States Historical Division at Montgomery, Alabama.

The 305th Bombardment Group (Heavy) had been largely ignored by writers, so I turned my attention to their files. It was soon apparent their records were so fragmentary that I could only vaguely define the scope of their operations.

Prologue

I felt a kinship with them, however, because the group had no shining symbols, no celebrated heroes, and little publicity during the wartime years, although they had achieved an unmatched record of accomplishment.

The more I studied the secret records, the more I felt compelled to know them better. The precise files contained all the facts and figures. It was obvious the group had been operated efficiently, just like a business. There was no aura of "flying circus" about the 305th.

Although the records were accurate and individual remembrances of events were vivid, a big question mark remained in my mind. What was the driving force behind these men which carrried them through the most incredible hardships any group of men had ever experienced?

On my way back to California, I accepted an invitation to visit the postwar home of the 305th.

They had been reactivated in January 1951. The 305th slowly took form again under Colonel Elliott Vandevanter, Jr., at McDill Air Force Base, Florida. Their first B-29 Superfortresses arrived in February, but they were outmoded World War II aircraft which were replaced later by modern jet bombers.

In October 1951, the wing was converted on paper from a B-29 to a B-47 wing. It wasn't until January, 1953, that the 305th finally achieved its long-awaited goal of becoming a combat-ready B-47 wing. January, 1954, marked the third anniversary of the 305th's reactivation. Prestige was added to the wing's "birthday party" by the presence of General Curtis E. LeMay, who returned to his old group to check out personally in the B-47. Typically, the wing received the Air Force Outstanding Unit Award for exceptional performance during these years.

Early in May, 1959, a B-47 touched down at Bunker Hill Air Force Base in Peru, Indiana, and the 305th moved into its new home. Colonel Frank L. O'Brien brought the first supersonic Hustler to Bunker Hill, a year later, and the 305th became the first Air Force unit to get the world's most devastating operational weapons system.

O'Brien, wing commander in the summer of 1961, greeted me at the entrance while I signed the base roster. He drove the staff car himself, keeping an attentive ear to the radio, while he explained the 305th's role as part of the Strategic Air Command.

I became acutely aware of his grave responsibilities while he spoke of the group's mission with qualities of decisiveness that reminded me of LeMay.

"This efficient base would make an industrialist proud," I said. "Many could learn from such an organization."

His handsome features lighted up momentarily. "You might call me a general manager of a highly technical and complicated organization," he said, "and the 'mayor' of a city of twelve thousand people with a payroll of more than one and a half million dollars a month."

I nodded. He already had explained that the taxpayers had an investment of $375,000,000 at Bunker Hill.

The neat homes and maintenance shops, the green lawns and the sound of happy children at play, were a far cry from Chelveston, England, I thought. Their wartime counterparts would be astonished by such comfortable surroundings after their memories of mud, cold, and war-weary bombers.

In my own mind, I knew that if they wondered whether their old outfit had grown soft with the peacetime years, they would be reassured after meeting the men of the new 305th.

It was evident to me that underneath this thin veneer of comfortable living, they belonged to the same breed of dedicated men who wrote a new definition of the word "courage" in the skies over Europe during World War II. After several hours with O'Brien, the feeling came over me that at last I had begun to understand these men. I felt certain that I had identified the shadow that gave substance to the wartime deeds of the 305th.

It started while we sat in O'Brien's office and our eyes fastened on the organization's shield behind his desk. I had seen the words many times before. Suddenly, they took on a new meaning and seemed a symbol of the inspiration, loyalty, and performance of all those who had ever served with the group.

Seeking the motivating force exemplified by LeMay and all the others, I had overlooked the obvious. I looked again at the shield. Those familiar words, which the Germans had learned to respect and the free nations to admire, told the story: "Can Do!" Simple, unaffected words, but strong with conviction and now underscored by achievement.

CHAPTER 1

"Boomtown's" Incredible Flight

AFTER SEVEN MISSIONS against Hitler's "Fortress Europe," LeMay knew something was wrong with his command. He could see it in the faces of the crew members around him. A sixth sense told him that the explosive forces which had been building up in his 305th Group during the past five frustrating weeks couldn't be contained much longer.

The briefing room was too quiet. His hazel eyes were troubled, belying his outward calm. A cloud of smoke ascended from his long cigar. He knew his men should be humming with nervous tension as they awaited word on their next mission. Instead, hundreds of upturned faces stared grimly as the operations officer, Lieutenant Colonel John H. de Russy, mounted the platform.

Major McGehee, sitting next to Colonel LeMay, said

soberly, "They can't take much more of this. They need a successful strike."

"I'm aware of it," LeMay said, more roughly than he intended. "It'll take time. We're all new at this."

Captain Clyde B. Walker sat stiffly on a bench with his "Boomtown" crew, his heart beating rapidly inside his flying suit. His hands opened and closed unconsciously as his face showed the strain of a fitful night.

His thoughts were of home back in Tulsa, Oklahoma, now that New Year's Eve was only two days away. He recalled the fun-filled holidays of the past, so unlike this tragic New Year's of 1943 which lay before them, offering no peace for mankind.

In a quiet voice, he said to his copilot, Lieutenant Reed, "World War II will never end unless we start destroying some targets."

Reed glanced nervously around the room. "We all need a good mission," he said. "I thought morale had reached bottom a week ago, but it is far worse now."

They snapped to attention as the curtain was drawn back and their mission route was exposed on the large map behind de Russy.

"Our target today is the German submarine pens at Lorient," de Russy said. "Major McGehee will lead the group. We are the last of the five groups participating in the mission. Here are the details."

When the crews heard the target heading, loud protests were voiced.

A pilot stood up. "We'll be making the run directly into the afternoon sun. We'll never see the German fighters in time to track them."

"I realize that," de Russy said, "but the route was

"Boomtown's" Incredible Flight

chosen particularly to keep away from heavily defeated flak areas. The route is a compromise."

No one was convinced, and crews exchanged worried glances. Many an eye looked at Group Commander LeMay who, dressed in flying clothes, sat with the crew of the lead aircaft in which he was going to ride as top turret gunner.

LeMay stood up. "A great deal of time and effort went into the planning of this mission," he said forcefully. "You can have the utmost confidence in the route we selected because flak should be more of a problem than fighters. I'm going along to find out for myself what particular problems are facing the gunners."

Walker and his crew had few words as they left the briefing room for the flight line and boarded their B-17 Flying Fortress. Their spirits were dampened even further by the drizzle and heavy overcast at the field.

Walker's confidence returned as one by one the four engines coughed briefly and then broke into an even roar of restrained power. He and Reed efficiently went over the check list.

"A low ceiling," Walker said. "Can't be over five hundred feet."

"Visibility is less than two miles," Reed said. "I'll be glad when we climb out of this soup and see the gun again."

One by one the group's planes roared down the runway at Chelveston and headed across the Channel from the southeast coast of England.

Walker, who had been listening to the radio, heard a coded call from the flight commander of the 364th Squadron.

"The 364th is returning," he said to Reed.

Tight lines appeared around the copilot's eyes. "How come?"

"They couldn't find us over the base during rendezvous. They tried to meet us at the start point, but we were already over the channel. They had no alternative."

"We'll miss their fire power over the target," Reed said.

Walker, in the left element, watched the tight formation with pride as they headed for the target. They hugged one another's wing tips protectively so their massed fire power could thwart the most ambitious Nazi fighters.

The lead plane weaved back and forth as Lieutenant J. J. Varhol leaned over his bombsight and carefully made his adjustments. The bombardier was relieved that visibility was perfect. The sub pens showed clearly below him. With a delicate last adjustment, he called excitedly, "Bombs away!"

The group's thirteen remaining B-17's salvoed, and twenty-six two-thousand-pound bombs dropped from sight.

Varhol watched for the impact. When the bursts spread throughout the area, he called, "Bull's-eye!"

His exultation faded fast when he saw a series of FW-190's coming toward him in line, with the leader's guns winking viciously.

After the first breathless attack, Walker and his crew thought the worst was over. They were wrong. Time after time, the enemy developed new attacks which they had never seen before. An FW would attack from one or two o'clock to draw the fire of the turrets, while a second and third attack would come from nine o'clock.

"Boomtown's" Incredible Flight 11

"Short bursts!" Walker called urgently. "Don't waste ammunition."

The words were no sooner out than "Boomtown" shook with a hail of flak and explosive bullets that almost blew the Fortress out of the sky.

"Bombardier from pilot. Are you all right?"

No answer. "Bombardier from pilot! Are you hurt?"

The intercom clicked, and a voice overcome with emotion said, "Navigator to pilot." There was another long pause. Then Lieutenant Smith said, "Bentinck is dead!"

Walker winced at the news. "Smith," he called. "Are you injured?"

"Only a piece of flak in the arm."

"Can you man the nose guns?" Walker said.

"I'll be all right," Smith said unsteadily.

Walker started to speak, but an explosive shell ripped the bottom out of the ball turret and the Fortress reverberated with the new shock.

Sergeant Green was blinded by oil and escaping fumes. With his oxygen destroyed, he gasped for air and every movement was a torture. In one panicked moment, he thought his left leg had been blown off, but despite his cramped quarters he saw with relief that the spare ammunition had jammed tightly against his leg.

"Pilot to Green. Are you hurt badly?"

"I'm okay. Shook up a bit, but I'm staying here to cover my area."

In the tail turret, Sergeant Krucher was badly hit. Despite painful wounds, the former clerk continued to man his guns. When an FW charged in on the tail, he shot half its wing off and watched it hurtle earthward.

Simultaneously, Sergeant Stroud destroyed another

enemy aircraft. The fighter attacked from in front, passing so close to the sights of his right waist gun that he could see the enemy pilot's head. With straining eyes and firm hands on the gun, Stroud watched the fighter approach from twelve o'clock. The fighter banked and started in on the tail, and Stroud let him have it. The Nazi fighter's fuselage ripped open and fell towards the sea.

The Fortress staggered away from the blistering attack while fighters came in pairs. The first attack had broken the drive shaft of the number one engine, and Walker struggled hard to control the Fortress. The second engine, which had been hit on one of the top cylinders, increased his problems because only emergency power remained.

Walker advanced the throttle slowly, but the prop started to run away. The oil pressure was dropping, but this was a minor problem compared with his other troubles. Flak had blown a large hole in the nose, the ball turret was shattered, the bomb bay doors were shot up by shell fire, and the de-icing system was punctured.

A quick check with crew positions told him the radio equipment was damaged and the elevator control cable had been knocked off its pulley.

"Copilot to pilot!"

"Yes, Reed, go ahead."

"Flak has destroyed my parachute!"

Walker, struggling to level the airplane, had time only for a shocked glance at his copilot. All thought of abandoning the battered airplane was thrust aside. There were clouds ahead, so he desperately tried to reach their protection for his hard-hit crew.

Despite the extreme cold in the cabin, sweat poured from Walker's face as he used every ounce of energy to

"Boomtown's" Incredible Flight 13

fly the airplane. With the utmost skill, using evasive action, he managed to elude the fighters.

Although Gunner Stroud had been hit by a .50-caliber bullet and the plane was plunging along on an uneven keel, he painfully slipped the elevator cable back on its pulley.

Walker had tried to keep up with the formation, but his Fortress lost altitude at the rate of two thousand feet a minute. At ten thousand feet, Sergeant Frisholz brought down a third enemy fighter with the blazing guns of his top turret.

Troubles mounted for the stricken crew as Frisholz had to leave his guns to put out a fire in the radio compartment. In the waist, Stroud and Sergeant Berring drove off two more 190's.

During a quiet moment, Walker looked out the window to notice that a Fortress from another group had come down to fly beside them.

"Thank God," Walker said, "we've got a friend."

"Boomtown" finally ducked into the temporary safety of the clouds. When they came out in the clear again, they were alone but still losing altitude at the rate of two thousand feet a minute.

Checking each station in the plane, Walker learned all crew members were at their positions except the dead bombardier and the wounded Krucher, who had been relieved in the tail turret by Stroud, himself wounded.

Smith grabbed Krucher with rough tenderness. "Lie down!" he ordered. He cut open Krucher's electric suit and quickly administered first aid.

Walker spotted land. "There's England," he shouted. "I'm heading right in."

Sergeant Green took one look at the land. "That don't

look like England to me." He was right. They saw before them the very sub pens they had bombed once before, and they knew it was Brest.

By this time, the B-17 was down to six thousand feet and still losing altitude. Roaring directly over the harbor, they passed numerous merchant ships.

Walker hastily cut across the open Channel, passing directly between two destroyers who were too astonished to open fire.

They now were flying on two engines. Walker's arms shook with nervous strain as the number two prop, which was out of control, threatened to wreck the airplane. Several times the ball turret bounced on the waters of the Channel despite his mightiest attempts to keep the airplane straight and level.

Reed said flatly, "I hope it will jar that propeller loose."

Stroud yelled, "Chief, you're doing that just to gain altitude on the bounce!"

"It helps," Walker said with a forced grin. "We come up a hundred feet each time."

Their situation becoming even more precarious, Walker called the crew, "Prepare for a crash landing at sea! Heave everything out that isn't bolted down."

They took him literally and threw out ammunition, oxygen bottles, masks, parachutes, everything.

When the last article was gone, Frisholz yelled, "Two fighters overhead. Where's my ammunition?"

Berring stood there resolutely and just shrugged his shoulders.

Walker's pulse seemed to stop as he searched the sky for fighters. He said a silent prayer of thanksgiving when they didn't attack.

Time after time Walker was ready to ditch, but every time the crew braced for the crash, he managed to increase the plane's altitude a few more feet.

With extraordinary skill, Walker finally managed to pull the bomber up eight hundred feet, and they crossed safely over the English coast and landed soon after at a British base.

British crews helped them down and took charge of Bentinck's body. Then, crazed with relief, the crew swarmed around Walker and pounded him hysterically. They tried to tell him how his flying saved their lives.

Walker said merely, "You guys deserve all the credit."

"How about Stroud?" Reed said with awe. "He's high gunner now, with four destroyed and one probable. Funny part of it is he never went to gunnery school. He's a bombardier."

LeMay was exhausted from the mission and sat down heavily at his desk. He was saddened by the losses the group had suffered.

Going over the mission in detail, it was obvious that a more definite plan of return should have been incorporated in the orders. Leaving the decision to the last minute added immensely to the difficulty of reassembly after the attack.

He had to remind Operations, also, that crews must remain at their combat stations until the planes returned to the base. The surprise attack off Brest on their return caught many crew members away from their combat stations.

When he studied the report of the incredible flight of Walker's crew, he felt a warm glow for their courage and endurance under impossible conditions. For the first time, he felt truly confident that he had a real fighting organization in his hands which could take on the best of the Luftwaffe any time and any place.

He noted the attack had seen forty of the seventy-seven B-17's reach the target. It was evident the bombs were well placed and that many hits had been scored on the target area, although the impregnable underground pens had not suffered appreciable damage.

LeMay smiled as he read a wire from Captain E. E. Tribbett, who had brought his badly damaged bomber to an emergency landing several miles from home base.

It was brief, to the point. "Bombed target," Tribbett wired. "Ship badly shot up."

"Sergeant!" LeMay called.

"Yes, sir."

"Tell Colonel de Russy and Major Green I want to see them right away."

All lingering doubts about the fighting caliber of the 305th Bombardment Group, which he had brought to England from the States, were erased. He knew, however, that despite the meticulous training they had had in their B-17F Flying Fortresses since the group's activation on March 1, 1942, they had seen only the beginning of many supreme tests.

The air of his austere office was blue with cigar smoke as he leaned back. As he thought of the young men under his command, he knew in his heart that, despite fears, uncertainties, and lack of combat experience, the Luftwaffe could never turn them back. He recalled Goering's boast that no American bomber would ever penetrate the Reich, but he knew his own men better than the German Marshal did.

Major Charles A. Green, group Intelligence officer,

stepped into LeMay's office. "You ought to be in bed, Curt," he said. "You've had a rough day."

LeMay brushed the idea aside with a wave of his hand.

"Sit down. It's time we had another talk." He leaned forward. "The preliminaries are over. The crews have had some combat experience but they have a long way to go before they become proficient in their jobs."

"This has been a frustrating month. The group..."

"I know. We've all got to prove ourselves. I am well aware of the doubts of those who think daylight bombing of Germany is suicidal. Let me tell you something," he said vigorously. "You and I will see the time when thousands of bombers will hit Fortress Europe. Airpower will do much to decide World War II," he said decisively.

"I agree," Green said. "Don't expect too much right now. After all we're only one of five heavy bomber groups in England. That's a small striking force."

"It's all we can spare at this critical time," LeMay said practically.

He looked up as de Russy walked in. "I know it's late, John, but I've got some things to go over while they're fresh in my mind."

"What did you think of today's mission?" de Russy said.

"It's the turning point in our operations," LeMay said. "That's my main reason for getting the three of us together."

He paused. "Let's look at the record to date. Perhaps it will give us some ideas for bettering our performance. That first mission on November 17 served primarily to give the crews experience on a combat mission. Inasmuch as it was an unsuccessful diversionary sweep to draw defenders away from the strike by Eighth Air Force bombers against the U-Boat base at St. Nazaire, no important lessons were learned."

"It failed its primary purpose only because no enemy fighters were encountered," de Russy said.

"The same thing can be said for the diversionary sweep the following day," Green added.

"We gained experience over enemy territory," LeMay said stubbornly.

"We could have had a good mission on November 23," Green said, "if it hadn't been for the weather over Lorient."

"Cloud cover at the target is a fact of life we'll have to learn to live with," LeMay said.

"Our missions have not all been in vain," de Russy said defensively. "The crews performed well through intense flak over St. Nazaire on the twenty-fourth. Fourteen out of our sixteeen planes claimed hits on the German U-Boat base."

"I know that," LeMay said. Then the smoke from his cigar came rapidly in strong puffs as he pointed a finger at de Russy. "We had our best chance to score effective hits when we bombed the locomotive and carriage works at Lille."

The Operations officer nodded. "I realize only four planes dropped bombs on the target, but the other sixteen had difficulty picking up the target."

LeMay's face was set in grim lines. "It cost us a crew when Lieutenant Prentice was shot down over Tournai."

"They had an engine failure," de Russy said. "An FW-190 was hit by the plane, and both the B-17 and its attacker disintegrated in midair."

"How did we stack up with the 91st and 303rd Groups on that mission?" LeMay demanded.

"Very badly. The 91st sent twenty-two aircaft and eighteen of them attacked the target. The 303rd had fifteen over the target out of twenty taking off."

"We've got serious problems," LeMay said. "Perhaps more than I realized. When you take young men right out of school, with a minimum amount of training, and expose them to the best pursuit and antiaircraft defenses in the world, it takes time to make them a fighting team."

"Navigation has been difficult," Green said.

"I realize that. Without exception, our navigators are weak in pilotage, especially over this type of terrain. At home a railroad, town, or river is a check point. Over here the landscape is one jumbled mass of railroads, roads, and towns. Once you lose track of your position, it is almost impossible to find yourself again. I'm putting them back in school," he said. "I won't have a repetition of what happened at Lille."

"There are some situations which are beyond our control," de Russy said. "Look what happened over Rouen-Sotteville. Complete cloud cover obscured the target. You can't expect the men to bomb a target under such conditions."

"I know, I know," LeMay said impatiently, "but we had a chance December 20 when we attacked the enemy airfield at Romilly-sur-Seine. The results of that mission were unbelievably bad despite the fact the Eighth Air Force had eighty-three heavy bombers over the target."

They agreed.

"Now listen to me, both of you. I accept full responsibility for what has happened. We've all got a lot to learn, but we'll only improve by recognizing our mistakes."

He looked at them intently. "We've got an impossible

job," he said. "If we all work together, it can be done. I'll talk to you some more in the morning. Right now I've got some letters to write."

Green looked at LeMay, noting the lines of fatigue on his face. "The letters can wait until tomorrow, Curt."

"No, they can't," LeMay said. "We lost ten men today, and their families have a right to know as soon as possible."

Green looked at his commander. Although the colonel quickly turned away, Green was astonished to find in the eyes of his tough boss the unmistakable signs of tears.

"Good night, Curt," Green said, as both he and de Russy withdrew.

CHAPTER 2

The Cabin Seemed to Explode

GREEN WAS SURPRISED to find LeMay alert in mind and spirits as he entered the colonel's office the following morning. "You couldn't have slept long."

"Long enough," LeMay said.

Colonel de Russy walked in. LeMay waved them to chairs in front of his desk. He leaned back, methodically stuffing a long pipe with tobacco, and lit up.

His eyes were alive with the thoughts inside him. "I've come to a decision," he said abruptly. "Our losses are far too heavy for the minor gains we are achieving. We've got to change the tactical doctrine."

"What do you have in mind?" de Russy said.

"Our pilots are excellent. There are none better. All of them, however, are weak in formation flying particularly at altitudes under full-load conditions."

"They are still inexperienced, Curt. You're not being fair. Give them a chance."

LeMay inhaled deeply and contemplated the cloud of bluish smoke as it rose to the ceiling. "These are my boys, John," he said quietly. "I know every one of them. We took them fresh out of flying school, sent them through three quick phases of training, and shipped them over here. They entered combat a year before they were ready. Now they are here," he said a trifle harshly, "they've got a job to do and it's up to me to see they do it. I want as many of them to live through this as is humanly possible. This won't happen if we continue our present tactics."

"I'm trying to be realistic," de Russy said. "What can we do?"

LeMay removed the pipe from the corner of his mouth. "Let's look at it logically. Our pilots know how to fly a normal six-plane squadron formation. That's suicide over here, where the Germans concentrate on one ship in a small formation, cut it out, and shoot it down."

"If we only had weather for training missions," Green said soberly, "we could whip this problem in two weeks."

"We're lucky to have enough decent weather for a combat mission," de Russy said bitterly.

"That's the point," LeMay said. "We've got to adapt our tactics to match their capabilities." He leaned forward eagerly, and his square face throbbed with suppressed excitement. "I've decided to modify our present formations and fly the squadrons at varying altitudes in an eighteen-plane group stagger. This will give a greater depth of formation and allow the turrets to fire at fighters making head-on attacks. While I've been on missions myself and checked the records of the others, I've learned

The Cabin Seemed to Explode

that 80 per cent of all attacks are head-on and level from twelve o'clock."

At first de Russy wasn't convinced, but the more he thought of the idea the more it appealed to him. "This would make it difficult for the Germans to bluff their way through a formation and break it up," he said. "I've noticed lately this is one of their favorite tactics."

"I have too. I'm proud of the boys because they didn't bluff so easily. This is not the perfect answer to the problem," LeMay said. "Ideally, each formation should consist of twelve airplanes. We'll come to that later. At this stage, the group stagger is the best answer."

"It should help the bomb pattern," de Russy said. "We've been throwing bombs everywhere but on target."

"Our bombing has been terrible," LeMay said. "Not just with us but in the Eighth Air Force. John, do you realize that 60 per cent of the bombs dropped can't even be accounted for? Let me show you something." He searched quickly through a thick file of reports. "Here it is. Listen to this. Less than 1 per cent of the bombs hit the aiming point, and only 3 per cent are within five hundred feet."

"Our bombardiers are good," de Russy said, "but they were trained under conditions where all they had to do was synchronize. Over here fighters are forcing attacks and sometimes the flak is so thick outside their plexiglass windows they could walk on it. There's no substitute for experience, Curt!"

"Yes, there is," LeMay said emphatically. "With the new stagger formation, I plan to advocate bombing by groups. This will give much needed protection at the target and place greatest reliance on the most talented bombardiers in the outfit. I keep reminding myself that there are many piano players but only one Paderewski."

"I'm sold," de Russy said. "When do we start?"

"Right away. I've been told the group will concentrate during January and February on anti-submarine campaigns with strikes against the sub pens at Lorient, Brest, and St. Nazaire. Targets such as these will give us time to develop our new techniques so we'll be ready later for the deep penetrations."

LeMay faced the crews on the morning of January 13 dressed for combat. He noted the buzz of excitement and the expectant faces looking up at him with satisfaction.

"You'll be happy to know," he said with a fleeting smile and a voice that carried strongly to the rear of the briefing room, "that we have proved our theories about defensive formation flying to the wing."

Loud cheers broke out, and LeMay's stern face relaxed. They quieted down quickly when he said, "We're leading the 1st Bombardment Wing on today's mission against the Fives-Lille Steel and Locomotive Works." They yelled louder than ever, but he waved them down impatiently. "All groups will use our procedure of group bombing instead of splitting into smaller squadron flights. Major Taylor will lead us, and I'll be along on Major Preston's crew."

Taylor's strong hands on the wheel had the sureness of experience as he pulled back and the Fortress lifted cleanly off the ground at exactly 11:30 A.M.

Twenty-two more of the group's planes followed him, although one later had to abort.

Haze and clouds covered the IP, and Lieutenant Gardner, in the bombardier's seat, glanced anxiously through

The Cabin Seemed to Explode

the plexiglass nose to spot the target.

"Bombardier to pilot. We're a little to the right of our planned course."

"Can you see the target?" Taylor said anxiously.

"I see it."

"It's up to you. Remember, no evasive action, just a straight course to the target."

Gardner clicked the interphone to signify he understood. He carefully adjusted his bombsight for five tremulous minutes, while over two hundred men in the formation waited impatiently, scanning the sky with anxious eyes for enemy fighters.

Flying at twenty-two thousand feet, Gardner sighted for both range and deflection. All the other bombardiers concerned themselves only with range.

"Fighter! Three o'clock, low!"

The gunner's voice cut through the silence in Taylor's airplane, while faces tensed up and eyes reflected their anxious concern.

Taylor looked at Boyle in the copilot's seat. "Not much flak, and the German's fighters aren't aggressive."

Guns chattered briefly but in a desultory fashion.

"This is too good to last," Boyle said nervously.

"Bombs away!" Gardner yelled.

Then a lone FW-190 came in, weaving from side to side, level and at eleven o'clock. They were taken by surprise, but all guns quickly were brought to bear as the fighter pressed relentlessly on towards the formation, firing steadily.

Boyle felt the shock of bullets tearing through the tail and wing of the B-17 and winced with pain as a shell fragment penetrated his right leg.

Suddenly, the cabin seemed to explode. Boyle looked

quickly at the pilot but recoiled with horror when he saw that Taylor had been killed instantly by a 20 mm. cannon shell that had smashed through the pilot's window.

The aircraft went into a wild dive, falling two thousand feet.

Boyle froze momentarily as he thought the engines had been shot out. Noticing Taylor's body slumped over the controls, he quickly realized that the weight of his body had forced the control column forward. Unfastening his seat belt, he struggled madly against the forces of gravity to get out of his seat. His hands shook, and his whole body trembled with exertion as he pulled Taylor's body away from the controls.

Every movement was an extreme effort, and he flopped hurriedly into his seat, his breath coming in deep gasps, and pulled mightily on the control column. The airplane responded slowly to his mightiest efforts, and the muscles in his arms knotted in firm cords. He breathed a sigh of unutterable relief as the plane leveled off.

Now that the aircraft was out of formation, swarms of German fighters descended upon it to make a quick kill.

Boyle now had regained mastery of himself, but the airplane was riddled with bullets through the nose, the top turret, and the ball turret.

"All positions," Boyle called. "Report injuries."

It was only then he learned that Sergeant Beach and Sergeant Hill had been injured in the legs.

Boyle struggled to keep his voice calm. "Taylor has been killed," he said with authoritative tones. "We'll fight our way out of this if each of you does his part. I need help from two of you to move Taylor's body out

The Cabin Seemed to Explode

of the pilot's compartment. Who can help?"

Beach replied. "I'll be right up."

"You're wounded," Boyle said. "Let someone else come up."

"I'm okay," Beach said. "Besides the others are busy."

He and Ballew, the radio operator, hurried to the pilot's deck. They gently removed the pilot's body from his seat and carried him to the nose section.

In the meantime, Sergeant Hill winced with extreme pain as a bullet pierced his thigh while he operated the guns in the ball turret.

When Boyle learned his condition, he called urgently, "Sergeant Mabry! Help Hill out of the turret."

Although weak, Hill's voice was firm. "I'm staying here as long as fighter attacks continue."

"That's an order," Boyle called. "Get him out, Mabry!" His voice softened. "Good work, Hill."

Beach had returned to his position at the top turret guns, so Ballew administered first aid to the injured Hill.

Boyle was appalled by the savagery of the attack. It was unbelievable and it seemed impossible the rugged Fort could withstand anymore. He flinched as new cannon shots smashed into the nose, fuselage, cockpit, and tail.

Boyle checked the radio, but, to his consternation, he found it was completely dead except for interphone communication between him and the tail gunner and the navigator.

With eyes that roved the sky intently, he saw a fighter bore in, and then cannon shells burst in the nose. He suspected the worst, but only the oxygen masks were blown off the faces of his bombardier and navigator. He listened anxiously for their guns and was momentarily relieved to hear continuous firing emanating from their section.

Boyle finally managed to get the aircraft back into formation, taking the lead position of the second element of the number two squadron.

A minute later, Beach in the top turret felt a sharp pain in his left leg, and he struggled frantically to find his oxygen mask which had been blown off when a cannon shell pierced the turret.

Without oxygen, he could feel the lightheadedness that came from lack of life-giving air at high altitudes. Fighters forced their attacks so he forgot everything and kept the turret roaring as .50 calibre bullets shot from the turret in a steady stream.

Ballew, after putting a splint on Hill's leg, noticed Beach's plight, so he and Mabry helped him out of the turret and gave him first aid.

When Mabry was done, he took a look in the cockpit. "Need any help?" he said.

"I can use some," Boyle said grimly. "Can you be spared back there?"

"I think so."

"Get in the pilot's seat and give me a hand."

The attacks seemed to go on endlessly. Tail Gunner Willis, who had been firing constantly, found to his astonishment that the shoulders of his flying suit had been blown away by bullets during one vicious exchange. His parachute, he noted with dismay, had been riddled by flak.

Boyle's leg now pained him so it was almost unbearable. Although he didn't remember how it happened, the blood streaming from his face came from wounds he

The Cabin Seemed to Explode

had suffered in one of several battles with the enemy.

Finally, the attacks ended and they were over the Channel bound for England.

"The hydraulic system is out," Mabry said. "It will be a rough landing."

Boyle nodded understandingly. "After what we've been through, this is a minor problem," he said with a voice that shook audibly.

After landing back at Chelveston, the crew watched with tears in their eyes as Boyle was gently removed from the airplane. He was not an experienced pilot, but they all knew that his courage, levelheadedness, and ability in bringing their Fortress back had saved their lives.

The interrogating officers heard a lot about the yellow-nosed FW's from the crews.

Mabry voiced a universal feeling. "The 'Abbeville Kids' are the best we've run up against," he said emphatically. There was a note of grudging admiration in his voice that made a profound impression on the interrogators.

Although the gunners claimed twenty-nine enemy planes, this was scaled down realistically to proven claims of six destroyed, six probables, and seven damaged.

LeMay grabbed the strike photos as soon as the wet prints were developed. His eyes roved professionally over the tiny splotches of white indicating the bomb impacts.

He turned to de Russy. "The pattern is only two thousand feet wide so the formation held together properly. It appears that much damage was done. Look here, the steel and iron foundries and the forging plant are damaged."

The operations officer scanned the photographs eagerly. "The main group of workshops have suffered additional damage since previous strikes. It looks like there is severe damage to the Dufour Spinning Mill. Take a look, Curt. The main building appears to be almost completely destroyed."

Later on, after LeMay had discussed the mission with wing headquarters, he told de Russy, "The new formations undoubtedly put a higher percentage of bombs on the target at far less cost in crews than any previous missions."

"Sure tough about Tom Taylor," de Russy said sadly.

LeMay nodded in silent agreement.

"I think we're on the right track," de Russy said. "How do you feel about it?"

"On the whole, the operation was a success," LeMay said. "We lost Lieutenant Hilbinger's crew, but that's something we'll have to get used to. It will be a long war," he said sadly.

"We lost the only crew to enemy action," de Russy said. "That seems to indicate the new formation protects the following groups."

"They concentrated on us," LeMay said grimly. "We can expect that from now on." He paused thoughtfully, and his features set in rigid lines. "We've just got to have nose turrets! The majority of attacks are head-on, and we can't meet them with hand-operated machine guns. They are almost worthless."

"I agree. I understand the new B-17G's will have chin turrets. It will take months to get them," he said with regret.

"You have to fight a war with what you've got,"

The Cabin Seemed to Explode   31

LeMay said bluntly. "Right now we have a fine airplane that can stand incredible punishment. Like all military weapons, it has its weak points. With the B-17, it is weak defensive power in the nose. You have to hand it to the Germans. It didn't take them long to wise up to this fact and make the most of it."

CHAPTER 3

"Bail Out! Bail Out!"

"I HAVE A COPY of the memorandum by Brigadier General H. S. Hansell, our 1st Bombardment Wing Commander," LeMay told the staff, "in which he comments on the Lille operation to the commanding general of the VIII Bomber Command."

They leaned forward eagerly while the colonel puffed excitedly on his cigar.

"Air discipline, Hansell says, was greatly improved by using the newly standardized stagger formation." LeMay looked up at them with satisfaction. They nodded appreciatively. "He says the formations followed their projected itinerary precisely on time, up to the initial point, and the two combat wings were close enough to obtain the benefits of defensive position."

LeMay put the paper down for a moment. "I know you're all fed up with my harping on tight formations.

It paid off again because our lead group repeatedly fought off attacks by an estimated thirty to forty fighters using the same tactics used at St. Nazaire."

"They attacked in strings of two to four," de Russy said, "then flew parallel with the formation, turned about a mile in front of it, and attacked individual airplanes from slightly below and almost directly on the nose."

"Hansell says our new formation has provided a very large element of security for the groups following the lead group. He says it appears well suited to meet frontal attacks."

"We still need turret guns in the nose," de Russy said. "Any word how the modification work is proceeding at Honington?"

LeMay shook his head. "They've got their problems too," he said.

"The bombing left much to be desired," Major Green said.

"Hansell cites a number of causes," LeMay said. "One of them is a consistent and systematic shortage in current bombing, which he thinks is due to the type of bombing tables we are using. He has called for a thorough investigation of the tables to determine if they are in error."

"Do you honestly think the tables are wrong?" de Russy said doubtfully.

"I do not!" LeMay said emphatically. "Hundreds of thousands of dollars were expended on their preparation. It is inconceivable to me that they could be wrong. I'm more inclined to think the error is a human one despite the consistency of the reports."

"What about specific damage?" Green said.

"The analysis shows the majority of the bombs have been accounted for," LeMay said. "That's an improvement, at least," he said wryly. "Most of them are grouped in one area, and the total damage is greater than past performances. Here again, however, precision on the aiming point leaves much to be desired."

"Did Hansell take any cognizance of our criticism on the inadequacy of fighter support?" de Russy said.

"As you know," LeMay said, "I joined with other group commanders about the necessity of fighter accompaniment literally with or under bomber formations to cover frontal attacks. We were adamant such fighter support would make a tremendous difference in our capacity to withstand fighter assaults."

They nodded their heads in complete agreement. "Did we get the usual run-around?" Green said.

"Hansell assured us that conferences are under way with the fighter commands to discuss tactics and techniques for such operations. I am not critical of the fighter groups. I believe the fault lies more with the type of short-range aircraft they now have."

January 23 the group dispatched twenty-two aircraft to attack Lorient. When the lead plane's bombsight failed temporarily on the bomb run, the group went on to the secondary target at Brest.

Flak at both targets was accurate but more intense at Brest. Again enemy planes, both 190's and ME-109's, intercepted during the bomb run but without the aggressiveness they had shown in the past.

Bombing results were obscured by cloud cover, but some hits were seen on a jetty in the dock area. Claims of enemy aircraft resulted in awards of two destroyed, one probable and one damaged.

During the 305th's first mission to Germany, the "Can

Do" group attacked the U-Boat and shipbuilding facilities as a secondary target in the Wilhelmshaven area on January 27. Hits were made in the general area of Bauhofen, but bombing was made difficult by cloud cover. The flak was inconsequential, but enemy fighters harassed the formation and the gunners claimed several of them.

An abortive mission was flown against Emden February 4 when no bombs were dropped due to clouds.

The Germans guarded their treasured submarine pens at St. Nazaire with intense and accurate flak on February 16 when eleven of the fifteen aircraft of the group were hit.

In a mission led by the 306th Group, several direct hits were made while enemy fighters attacked aggressively. Sometimes they followed each other closely, making circles and attacking at each round.

Not one bomb of the 305th landed on the target because the lead bombardier learned too late his bombsight wasn't functioning properly. The trouble should have been detected earlier, but it was not apparent until it was too late to warn the deputy bombardier to take over.

LeMay's cigar rotated like a pin wheel, and his voice was unusually gruff when he called in de Russy. "We lost two crews, Captain Steenbarger, and Lieutenant Burman, and not one bomb on the target!"

Although his voice was low, it cut like a knife in the electric atmosphere of his office. This was no time for apologies, so the operations officer merely nodded his head soberly.

"From now on," LeMay said bluntly, "see that each bombardier checks his sight thoroughly before reaching enemy territory."

The operations officer started to speak but he was cut

short. "I want the bombardiers trained in maintenance of the bombsight," LeMay said curtly, "and from now on they are solely responsible both for the maintenance and operation of their bombsight. Is that clear?"

"Yes, sir," de Russy said. He saluted and quickly withdrew.

Major J. J. Preston relaxed after take-off on February 26. The smooth roar of the engines told him all was well for the time being.

"There's our landfall," he called to his bombardier. "We're on course."

Lieutenant C. J. Malec gazed out of the nose of his B-17 at the Frisian Islands below him.

"Everything is going well," Preston said to his copilot. "No early returns," he said with satisfaction as his eyes roved the sky and checked the formation.

After Baltrum Island disappeared behind them, their alertness increased. Bombardier Malec called the pilot. "Cloud cover spreads across the entire area of the primary at Bremen," he said anxiously. "We'd better try for the secondary at Wilhelmshaven."

"Roger."

Preston slowly turned to the left and established a heading from the south. He and Captain Breeding in the copilot's seat exchanged solemn glances.

Malec's voice sounded shrilly over the intercom and betrayed his nervousness. "Secondary also covered from this heading!"

"This maneuvering over enemy territory is asking for trouble," Preston said as his hands clutched the control column.

"Enemy fighters must be alerted by now," Breeding

said with a catch in his voice. "I'll bet they have us pinpointed."

"Fighter! Twelve o'clock, high!"

The guns roared as single attacks came in waves with the Germans taking advantage of the sun at their backs.

Malec saw instantly there was too much cloud cover to get an accurate sighting on the submarine yards. Although the aiming point was obscured, a few breaks in the clouds gave him a chance to synchronize on check points and the bombs went away.

"The flak is wicked!" Preston said breathlessly.

"No fighters will bother us here," the copilot said.

"Wait 'til we get beyond the target," Preston said grimly. "They'll be back."

Meanwhile, one of the wing ships, piloted by Lieutenant Ashcraft, sustained a hit that shattered the navigator's compartment. Lieutenant Moberly was stunned momentarily when the overhead burst slammed down on top of him and only his steel helmet saved him from death.

They knew they were in for it, and they clung together protectively to fight their way out. The heavy barrage of flak continued, and they had no choice but to wait desperately until they were out of range of those murderous guns on the ground.

Preston watched helplessly as the bombardier and navigator on Lieutenant Adam's crew bailed out hastily over the target when a shell penetrated their compartment. The blinding flash told him all too well that an oxygen bottle had exploded.

Although Preston's eyes roved the sky, neither he nor any one else noticed the tragedy as Captain Tribbet and

"Bail Out! Bail Out!"

Lieutenant Benson were shot down in the heat of combat.

"Fighters! Twelve o'clock, level," the top turret gunner screamed.

Two ME-109's made repeated attacks on Lieutenant Stallman's plane on the far side of the right element. They fought back tenaciously as flak hit the tail gunner, the right wing, and the number four engine, knocking them out of formation.

While Stallman fought to master the crippled Fortress, he felt the shock of heavy flak hit them. Trying with all his might to regain the protective custody of the formation, he quickly realized the plane was too badly damaged.

Staff Sergeant Lee C. Gordon was cut by flying glass and fragments until blood cascaded down his face in a steady stream.

The plane was uncontrollable. Sallman yelled, "Bail out! Bail out!"

"Shorty" Gordon rolled out of his ball turret and almost immediately opened his parachute at twenty-four thousand feet. The silk streamed out behind him, and he felt a terrific jolt. He had forgotten to adjust the straps tightly.

Flak burst all around him. He watched intently as a German fighter came towards him only to turn up on one wing and fly on.

When his parachute opened, his flying boots, electric shoes, and gloves had been jerked off. The penetrating cold was so severe he had to beat his feet and hands together to keep warm. He was furious at himself for opening his parachute at such a high altitude.

Drifting down over the bay southeast of Wilhelmshaven, he broke through the clouds and saw a breakwater with stakes along the edge of the bay. The next thing he knew he hit the ground with a teeth-rattling jar. When the parachute began to drag him over the stakes, he disentangled himself, walked painfully a few feet in the mud, and stopped to examine himself.

He was quickly captured, but, with the indomitable courage of a man who refused to accept imprisonment, he soon started the first of a long series of unsuccessful attempts to escape from German prison camps until the final triumphant escape brought him safely back to England more than a year later.

LeMay's cigar was at a confident angle as he said to de Russy, "We did a lot better getting planes over the target this time."

"Our losses were bad, but evidently enemy opposition has been strengthened, particularly the concentration of both flak and fighters in this area. I imagine this is due to the fact the R.A.F. has struck the target repeatedly within the last two weeks."

"The bombing results were negligible, but I realize the bombardiers couldn't sight properly with the aiming points obscured by clouds. This will continue to be a serious problem until radar bombing can be perfected."

"Three men report frozen feet. The temperature was minus forty degrees centigrade at flight altitude, and the electric shoes are not adequate for such extreme temperatures."

"That's another problem we've got to solve," LeMay said wearily.

• • •

"Bail Out! Bail Out!"

After being recalled on February 27, without dropping any bombs, the group didn't fly again until it turned its attention to Holland on March 4 with an attack on Rotterdam. Twelve B-17's bombed with only fair results because most of the bombs fell in a canal near the aiming point.

Two days later, the group bombed the power plant at Lorient. The two groups which preceeded the 305th got considerable flak, but, as they went over the target, it suddenly stopped.

During a strike against the Rennes Marshalling Yard March 8, photographs showed ten hits and considerable smoke and fire.

In reviewing the reports of the mission, LeMay called de Russy into his office.

"John, the crew reports on the last mission are quite similar in regard to fighter attacks. They appear to concentrate exclusively on the nose and, for the first time, reveal *a tendency to identify themselves as part of our own Allied escort.*"

"This is true," de Russy said. "About thirty enemy fighters, mostly 190's and 109's, used identical patterns. As a rule, three enemy planes flew as a flight with our Spitfires, weaving like our escort, then attacking. One of our B-17's evidently was caught unawares by this maneuver, and they crashed into the Channel."

"Mention it at the next briefing. I know they are alert under attack, but the Germans are always developing new techniques. We're up against the masters of them all," he said admiringly, "so we've got to be constantly on our toes."

"The crews appreciate the fighter support," de Russy

said. "This is the first time in several operations where they have seen them."

LeMay scanned the reports thoughtfully. "They all say the same thing," he said. "They credit the Spits with good support and say they engaged the Germans in many combats."

"I've already talked to the squadron commanders about maintaining combat discipline over the Channel," de Russy said. "The Germans followed them almost to England."

"How about the crew that landed at another base?"

"They're all right. A rough time, according to the pilot, who landed at the base with only one engine still functioning."

LeMay lifted a thoughtful eyebrow. "Send him in when he gets back. Any man who can perform such a feat deserves a personal commendation."

A refreshing change for the "Can Do" bombers occurred on March 12 when no enemy planes attacked during the run on the target at the Rouen marshalling yards.

The Spitfire escort was picked up before crossing the French coast and stayed with them until they were over the Channel. They managed to chase off five enemy aircraft to the rear of the group.

Only a few hits were scored on the yards. The low squadron hit gas and oil storage tanks, causing fires which sent smoke billowing up to twelve thousand feet.

Cloud cover again made bombing difficult on the thirteenth when Amiens was attacked. As the group left the target, the "Abbeville Kids" rose to the attack and a vicious encounter took place.

Again the crews were warm in their praise of the Spitfire escort. They told interrogators, "The sky was full of Spits. The 'Abbeville Kids,' for the first time, had difficulty developing attacks against us."

Lieutenant Ralph D. McKee jumped off the lorry in front of the barracks. He looked uncertainly at the happy throng waiting expectantly as the new crews gathered their luggage.

He heard a shout and glanced up curiously. "McKeegan!" he called with astonishment. "I didn't know you were with the 305th."

They shook hands warmly because this was the first time they had seen one another since pre-flight school.

"It's good to see a familiar face," McKee said.

"We're glad to see all of you," Rothery McKeegan said happily.

"Why?" McKee said curiously.

"You're the first replacements since we came to England. Lyle," he called to a grinning captain standing near by. "Here's your new navigator."

McKee's mouth dropped open. "New navigator? I'm already assigned to a crew."

"We lost both our navigator and bombardier over Wilhelmshaven so your crew has been broken up. From now on, you're flying with us," Lyle Adams said.

"Come on," McKeegan said. "I'll help you move in."

So much had happened to him in recent weeks that he followed meekly as they hauled his luggage into an open-bay R.A.F. building.

"It's on the rough side," McKeegan said, "but comfortable enough. How long have you been overseas?"

"Since January," McKee said. "We were supposed to be assigned to Air Force Headquarters in Iran, but the orders were changed and most of us came to England."

"We're in the 366th Squadron," McKeegan said. "It's a great outfit."

McKee looked doubtfully at his steel cot and its hard mattress. "Where's the shower room?"

"Shower room!" McKeegan said. "We don't have one. This is England, my friend. Coal is so scarce we can use only two inches of hot water in a tub to take a bath."

While McKee was hanging his blouse on the rack behind the cot, a sandy haired lieutenant sauntered over and, with great deliberateness, tried on the blouse.

McKee looked questioningly at McKeegan as the young lieutenant smoothed out the wrinkles and said, "It's a perfect fit." He turned to McKee and said with great seriousness, "It's unfortunate navigators rarely survive more than six missions. A death trap, that nose compartment, you know. I say, may I have the blouse after you go down?"

McKee swallowed tightly and looked with consternation at the solemn group clustered around him. "I . . ." He was too astonished to utter a word.

Someone tried to choke off a laugh, and that was all the group needed. They roared hysterically until the tears rushed down their cheeks.

"You're being hazed," McKeegan said in a voice still choked with laughter.

The uneasiness of joining a new group melted away, and he felt one of them for the first time since his arrival.

• • •

"Bail Out! Bail Out!"

LeMay was filled with excitement as he looked at the preliminary field order for March 18th. He called de Russy into his office.

"We've got a good one, John. It will give us a chance, weather permitting, to show what our seasoned crews can do on a daylight mission. God knows they need some success after all they've been through. Get them alerted, and make sure they are prepared for a real fight. Close the bar now and get them to bed early. They'll need all the stamina they can muster tomorrow!"

CHAPTER 4

A Magnificent Team

LEMAY FACED THE CREWS following the briefing. He waited until the room quieted down, aware of their intense faces, but also conscious that they were alert and ready for action.

"The submarine yards at Vegesack rank fifth in annual output among all the yards building U-Boats in Axis Europe," he said. Despite the pipe clenched in the corner of his mouth, his low voice carried distinctly to the farthest corner of the room.

"The fifty tons of bombs at your command can save countless ships and lives at sea. You have been thoroughly briefed and, if the target is clear, the bombardiers should have no difficulty spotting the seven slips. Let me reiterate what already has been mentioned," he said firmly. "Four of those ships are used to build five-hundred-ton submarines to harass the world's shipping lanes. They have a total capacity for making sixteen subs so their destruction will be a severe blow to Nazi Admirals."

He stepped down, and the crews hurriedly departed for their B-17's on the ramp.

McKee seemed so unconcerned as they boarded up that McKeegan looked at him doubtfully. "Aren't you nervous?"

"A little bit," McKee said. "I've been waiting to fly over Germany a long time," he said eagerly.

McKeegan looked at him as if he couldn't believe his ears. "I suppose this is just like a great adventure," he said sarcastically.

"Something like that," he said innocently.

"You'll learn," McKeegan said. "Right now you don't know enough to be afraid. Wait until the flak and tracers come at you. You won't think it's such a great adventure then!"

In the vicinity of the target, Lieutenant Williams, in the lead bombardier's seat, glanced intently through the plexiglass at the target ahead of him and twenty-six thousand feet below.

"Pilot to bombardier, over."

"Yes, sir."

"You're on automatic pilot. It's all yours!"

Williams clicked the switch of the intercom twice, signifying he understood.

While the formation gathered instinctively around the lead B-17, Williams went to work. There was a controlled nevousness to his fingertips as they gently moved the knobs of the bombsight to line up the seventeen plane formation with the target.

A Magnificent Team

He was still too far away for the final anxious moments of synchronization but he could clearly see the submarine yards at Vegesack.

He grimly set to work. The first groups had dropped their bombs, and he noted with satisfaction that they hit right on target.

Smoke now became a problem, but he had fixed the aiming point well in mind so he synchronized in front of the buildings and quickly moved the indices so the cross hairs in the telescope split the aiming point. He peered intently through the sight to detect any movement of the hairs. A touch on the rate knob and the indices crossed.

"Bombs away!"

A flak burst rocked the airplane.

"Check the damage!" Wangeman called.

Captain Schleeh, in the copilot's seat, looked out the window. Turning back to the pilot, he said, "Only a few holes in the wing."

Bombardier Williams leaned far over the sight and peered at the target below him. Smoke mushroomed from the fires started by the earlier groups. Then his bombs hit on the slips. He let out a whoop that brought a startled look to the navigator's face.

"What happened?" Lieutenant Tomeny said anxiously.

"We hit it!" Williams said exultantly.

Wangeman started a slow turn away from the target as German fighters flashed by.

"Pilot to bombardier. How'd we do?"

"You can take that one off the list!" Williams said excitedly.

"Good work!"

"How's the formation doing, Schleeh?" Wangeman said.

"They're tight and still with us. There are plenty of fighters, but they aren't aggressive."

"I've noticed that. The 'Abbeville Kids' must have stayed home today."

"I'm not sorry," Schleeh said soberly.

Back at base, McKeegan walked with McKee to the briefing room, noting the seriousness of his friend's face, and chuckled softly to himself.

"What's so funny?" McKee said sharply.

"How was the great adventure?"

McKee was about to retort violently but, noting the understanding in McKeegan's eyes, said, "The flak and fighters were a novelty at first, but I quickly realized it was serious business."

"It is," McKeegan said quietly. "Deadly serious business!"

"That's the best job of bombing we've done, Curt," de Russy said. "Intelligence tells me the raid was so successful that the yards will be of little value for at least twelve months."

"They are overly optimistic," LeMay said flatly, while smoke curled around his head from his pipe. Peering intently at the strike photographs, he said, "Of fifteen U-boat hulls on the slips, it may be that seven are damaged and I'm sure one has capsized on the slipway."

"I've got an early interpretative report that indicates the same thing. It also says that six others sustained slight damage and only two remain undamaged."

A Magnificent Team

"The plant and yards seem to show extensive damage," LeMay said, "although it is impossible to assess accurately from strike photographs."

"I agree," de Russy said. "The power house appears almost completely destroyed, the shipbuilding shops at the east end of the yard are two thirds destroyed, and those at the west end received four direct hits."

"It was a fine mission, John. I'm concerned, however, about the fuel problem. Your report says all aircraft were short of fuel when they came back."

"Three planes had to land before the formation," de Russy said, "and one landed at another base to refuel. That's cutting it too fine."

LeMay nodded. "We'll have to sacrifice some bomb tonnage on long flights in the future."

"Did you see the Eighth Air Force evaluation report?" de Russy said.

LeMay nodded slightly. "They say it was the most effective raid to date by United States bombers." LeMay puffed thoughtfully on his pipe. "Viewed from the combined angles of bombing results, successful defense against heavy fighter attack, and the strongest concentration of heavy flak yet encountered, it can be classified as a success."

"The crews did a magnificent job of defending themselves against heavy fighter attacks," de Russy said. "Along with the fighters, the flak was very accurate."

"We've got a magnificent team," LeMay said, looking de Russy full in the face. "For instances of individual heroism and devotion to duty in the face of death, today's mission to Vegesack is unmatched in the annals of the air war in Europe to date."

• • •

Later reports, after a thorough scientific scrutiny of the target had been completed, indicated this first estimate of the results was too optimistic. The bombing was accurate enough, but the damage to submarines under construction, and to plant facilities, was much less than the photographs seemed to indicate. Actually, a week's repair work enabled the yard to get back into production. Within six weeks its activities had returned virtually to normal.

There was an air of mounting suspense in the briefing room as de Russy stepped to the platform.

"Today we are leading an attacking force of four groups to bomb the Renault Works at Billancourt, Paris," he said, as the crews leaned forward. "This plant is the largest single producer of motor lorries in Axis Europe. It is almost self-contained, supplying the most of the parts and equipment used in the manufacture of trucks. Its destruction will assist greatly in the conduct of the German war effort."

He stepped down, and the group specialist went over the mission in detail.

Just before they departed for their aircraft, LeMay stood resolutely before them. "You may not realize it now," he said solemnly, "but I have a feeling April 4 is a day you will long remember. Your efforts are extremely important. Remember what we've told you and exert your utmost."

Major Wangeman pulled his B-17 off the ground at 11:10 A.M. In the nose, Group Bombardier Williams, the same bombardier responsible for the excellent bombing at Vegesack, checked his sight carefully while rendezvous was made with the 303rd Group.

All eighteen of the group's planes had joined the formation when they headed for Harwich. They made a brief diversion over the Channel to confuse the Germans and then proceeded to Beachy Head.

At Rouen, they were joined by Spitfires for support as they headed for Paris.

Wangeman turned to his copilot. "I don't understand it. We haven't seen a single enemy fighter."

"They'll be coming along," Schleeh said tightly.

The crew's eyes searched the sky for fighters as they approached the target.

The southwestern part of Paris lay below Williams, and, in the bright spring air, the target was clearly visible. He synchronized carefully, oblivious of the light flak bursting around him, and the bombs dropped.

Williams leaned over the sight to watch the impact. Paris looked beautiful, and he said to himself, "I'd sure like to see it on the ground some day."

The first bombs struck, and their massive explosive power slammed into the buildings, and it seemed to him as if the whole factory was engulfed in a rain of TNT.

"You plastered it, sir," Tail Gunner Sergeant Gifford said.

A cloud of smoke swirled skyward several thousand feet like a massive thundercloud.

They were exultant as they pulled away. "I can't believe it," Wangeman said. "Very little flak and no fighter opposition."

"Fighters! Twelve o'clock, level!"

Wangeman stared as if fascinated by the waves of

fighters flying three and five abreast roaring at them in head-on attacks. They concentrated on the low squadron, and the yellow-nosed Focke Wulfs pressed their attacks with such vigor that despite their own fears they had to admire their guts.

"We'll have to fight ourselves out of this one," Wangeman said breathlessly as another wave came towards them. "They're from Goering's squadron."

"Pilot to crew. Don't waste ammunitoin. You'll need every round before this is over."

The "cocktail kids" in "Dry Martini," leading the low squadron, were having the fight of their lives. Two shells crashed into the pilot's compartment, and the navigator's station but miraculously missed the men.

The navigator, Lieutenant James Moberly, watched carefully as a fighter circled the formation. When he was within a hundred yards, he fired a hundred and fifty rounds and the German's propeller flew completely off.

Captain Martini turned to his copilot with a grim-visaged face. "These Focke Wulfs may have yellow noses, but they don't fight that way."

Every gun fired continuously as Martini watched the deadly duel. There were so many claims being made that he couldn't believe it. Moberly, he recalled, claimed four, and he had heard as many as six others shouted over the intercom.

While the attack grew in ferocity, Martini took a quick look at the rest of the squadron. He was appalled when he found only three B-17's remained of the six he had started with.

"Check the numbers on your side," he said in a choked voice to Boyle.

A Magnificent Team

When they compared notes, they learned that Lieutenant Ellis, Lieutenant O'Neill, and Lieutenant Jones had gone down with their crews. It was a brutal loss that left both of them shaken.

The gunners still had a job to do or they wouldn't make it back either. Thousands of rounds poured out of the guns, but still the German fighters came in wave after wave singling out what was left of Martini's low squadron.

"Thank God for those twin nose guns," Martini said fervently to Boyle. Their squadron had been the first to have been installed.

"Without them," Boyle said, "our losses would be even worse."

It seemed an eternity before they reached the French coast and the fighters departed as the Spitfire escort joined them.

"Whew!" Martini said shakily. "I'm glad that's over. Goering must have given special orders to his boys today. They were out for blood!"

When the full story was revealed at base, it was learned that fifty combats had been recorded. Out of forty-eight aircraft claimed by all groups, the 305th was awarded twenty destroyed, six probables, and five damaged.

"Martini's gunners weren't exaggerating when they claimed ten fighters shot down," de Russy told LeMay.

"They had a brutal fight for their lives," LeMay said grimly. "It won't be the last."

Postwar investigation disclosed that eighty-one of the two hundred and fifty tons of high explosives were effective against the target and denied to the enemy approximately three thousand seventy-five trucks. In other words, this added up to thirty-eight trucks for each ton of bombs or the destruction of thirty-six trucks by each aircraft.

During a staff meeting, LeMay faced them with a confident air. "This is a great triumph for the American theory of daylight precision bombing. I have nothing but the warmest praise for all of you. Convey to the crews my high admiration for their skill."

"They are ready for anything," de Russy said confidently.

LeMay removed a cigar from his mouth, and his stern features relaxed. "I understand we have been recommended for a Distinguished Unit Citation for the group's extraordinary heroism," he said proudly.

"They deserve it," de Russy said.

LeMay nodded. "When you think how they fought off seventy-five fighters, the best of the German Air Force, it makes you proud to be an American. Without a doubt, this is the most successful operation carried out by bombardment forces in the European Theater of Operations."

"I hope someday people will appreciate what these men did this day," de Russy said. "Thirty officers and men paid the supreme price for decisively defeating the Germans in battle."

LeMay started to say something, but the words would not come. He hid his emotions behind a thick smoke screen of cigar smoke as the staff withdrew.

CHAPTER 5

A Day to Remember

BAD WEATHER WAS a boon to the exhausted crews during the rest of the month of April. It permitted only three more missions. These included the engine repair works at Antwerp, which were hit April 5 by eighteen planes of the group. Flak and fighter opposition was slight, and the bomb pattern extended across the railroad tracks and the eastern half of the plant. The crews deeply appreciated the fighter escort.

McKee lay back on his cot in their Nissen hut and idly watched a poker game in progress. The familiar strains of "The Waltz of the Flowers" filled the long bay as one of the officers put the record on for the seventh time that day. Its countless repetition day after day was getting on his nerves.

He could sense the build-up of tension since they were alerted for tomorrow's mission. He knew now what

McKeegan meant when he said before his first mission, "Right now you don't know enough to be afraid."

He did now after four missions in a month. The knowledge was in the strained faces of the young men playing poker, so reckless with money that McKee caught his breath in astonishment. He could appreciate why money had so little value. None of them were sure they would live to spend it.

McKeegan came over and sat on the side of his cot. "I wish these characters would knock it off," he said, pointing to the players. "I'm tired, and we've got a mission tomorrow."

"Number five for me," McKee said. "Isn't that some kind of milestone?"

"Not quite," McKeegan said. "Between the eighth and tenth you aren't sure you'll ever finish twenty-five missions alive. After you've sweat out number thirteen, you begin to feel like a pro and begin to hope there is a chance to finish the tour okay."

McKee sat up. "I'm new at this, but aren't the losses rather high?"

"Average," McKeegan said with a shrug. "They run about 8 per cent."

"Eight per cent!" McKee said. McKeegan watched him with amusement as he noted the mental arithmetic going on in his friend's mind. "Why that means," McKee said, wide-eyed with concern, "that you use up about 200 per cent of your chances on a twenty-five-mission tour."

"That's right. What do you want to do—live forever?"

McKee lay back, and McKeegan left him to his thoughts.

"Look, you guys," McKeegan said angrily to the poker

players. "It's time we all got some sleep. Now knock it off!"

They ignored him completely.

McKee sat up with astonishment as he saw McKeegan rush to his foot locker, pull out his service automatic, and fire at the lights.

They were so astonished that no one said a word. The crash of glass against the floor broke the silence in the darkened room. Then someone laughed, and the tension was eased.

When the "Can Do" Group went to Lorient April 16 to continue its string of attacks on the U-boat bases, the bombs fell on the aiming point and adjacent railroad. Inaccurate flak and ineffectual fighter attacks made it an easy mission for the battle-hardened crews.

The following day the Focke Wulf aircraft plant at Bremen was the target, and the bomb pattern covered the eastern half of the plant area with some bombs south of the factory. Again enemy planes were encountered over the Frisian Islands, attacking in pairs and taking advantage of the clouds above the group to achieve surprise. The 305th, however, was successful in keeping them off, ringing up a total of eleven destroyed during the mission. The flak was the most intense they had yet encountered. At the target, there was a box barrage from twenty-two to twenty-eight thousand feet and a half mile in depth. In spite of these obstacles, the group lost no planes.

Nine missions were carried out in May. The first, to St. Nazaire on the first day of the month, was fairly uneventful. On the fourth, however, enemy fighters tried a new type of attack.

LeMay called in de Russy. "How serious do you consider these new attacks where the Germans drop bombs from above on our formations?"

"It's rather a frightening experience for the crews," de Russy said, "but I don't personally feel there is any cause for alarm. The fusing is correct, and they burst at the proper altitude but well behind us, so no damage is suffered by this innovation."

"Fighter escort has improved tremendously," LeMay said with satisfaction. "Crews report they engaged German fighters in so many combats that they couldn't drive home their attacks against the bombers."

"I'm sure," de Russy said, "that their assistance explains in part the excellence of the bombing recently."

LeMay shifted a cigar idly around his mouth. "It helps to keep the Nazis off our backs."

Good bombing also was accomplished on May 13 in an attack on Meaulte by twenty-seven aircraft. Fighter support was good, although some fierce attacks were made by German fighters of which the group was credited with destroying six.

A mission to Kiel the next day resulted in thirty-one claims of enemy aircraft and awards of eleven destroyed. Bombing again was good, although some of the bombs hit to the right of the aiming point.

A mile and a half stretch of concrete lay before Lieutenant Whitson as he waited for the green light to start his roll. He sat stiffly in the pilot's seat, casually noting the black strips of rubber clinging to the cement, residue of countless landings.

A Day to Remember

The full roar of the four engines relaxed him as he released the brakes. The mounting suspense, which had been building up since the briefing, now subsided. With complete confidence, he lifted his Flying Fortress off the runway.

"It's good to be up here with the sun shining," he said to his copilot. "The endless drizzle gets on my nerves."

Lieutenant Holt nodded appreciatively. "Here we go again," he said. "One more to the list, and that much closer to 'Uncle Sugar.'"

Whitson listened closely to the engines as they crossed the coast of the continent. Their smooth throbbing increased his assurance in "Old Bill." He glanced up casually, and the muscles in his neck tightened. "Look overhead," he said to Holt.

The copilot was startled by the sight of streaming contrails at thirty-five thousand feet. "They can't wait until we get to the target today," he said tensely.

They had joined with the 303rd to form a composite striking force of two formations. The military installations at Wilhelmshaven had been assigned as primary target.

It soon became apparent to Lieutenant Barrall in the bombardier's compartment that bombing would be impossible.

"Bombardier to pilot, over."

"Go ahead."

"Primary completely covered by clouds."

Before Whitson could reply, he noticed fighters coming at them. "Pilot to crew. Here they come. Let 'em have it!"

An FW-190 raked the aircraft with 20 mm. shells.

Fragments slashed into Whitson's leg, and he cried out in pain.

Despite his wounds, he motioned to Holt to take over and grabbed a walk-around oxygen bottle so he could inspect the damage.

"You can't walk around with that bad leg!" Holt remonstrated.

"I've got to find out how serious the damage is," he said stubbornly.

With blood trickling down his leg, he painfully made his way inside the airplane. He was satisfied the situation wasn't serious yet so, being weak from loss of blood, he inched his way back to the pilot's seat.

Another swarm of twenty-five to thirty-five fighters struck at them, and FW-190's let go with everything they had, attacking from all angles, queuing on the damaged aircraft and pounding it with a barrage of 20 mm. shells and machine-gun bullets.

It seemed impossible to Whitson that the rugged ship could take such punishment. Just then, a 20 mm. shell burst through the cockpit window, and Whitson winced as he was wounded a second time. He glanced at Holt and, to his consternation, found his copilot was seriously wounded.

The whole plexiglass nose was shot away, and Lieutenant Venable, the navigator who had stayed valiantly at his post, was killed instantly.

Lieutenant Barrall saw an FW a split second before it fired and he threw himself behind the bombsight. Although he was painfully wounded by shell fragments, this quick action saved his life.

When the top turret splintered under the fierce enemy

A Day to Remember

attack, Sergeant Haymon also was wounded. Streaming blood from a gash in his head and a flak wound in his arm, he stayed in the useless turret desperately trying to get the Nazi fighters in his sights.

In the ball turret, Sergeant Nichols was wounded, and Sergeant Friend, along as a photographer, also was hit.

Whitson struggled to keep the shattered Fortress in formation, but, with the nose shot away, the right wing buckling, the hydraulic and oxygen systems shot out, the bomber dived away from the protective custody of the formation.

"All stations!" Whitson called urgently. "Report wounded."

He was appalled by what he heard. Only two of the eleven men aboard had not been hit.

Nazi fighters followed them down like a swarm of angry hornets, determined to destroy the stubborn Fortress.

Losing the defensive fire power of the group, the Fort appeared to be easy game for their flaming guns.

Ignoring their wounds, the gunners fought back out of a desperate desire to live. During their five-thousand-foot dive, Tail Gunner Sergeant Kenneth Meyer, who had escaped injury, made confirmed kills of three FW's in rapid succession.

Another 190 was sent spinning earthward, with pieces flying off it, by Sergeant John Breen in the waist. As the B-17 leveled off, Sergeant Nichols destroyed two more fighters with one of them blowing up spectacularly and going down like a "ball of fire."

The interphone was silent. The crew had too much on their minds to engage in talk. During the steep dive,

Sergeant Ramsay had been hurled against the top of the ship, lacerating his scalp. Recovering when the B-17 leveled off, he returned to his guns in time to destroy an FW sneaking in from seven o'clock, low. The fighter closed to three hundred yards before it exploded in flames, scattering debris over the sea.

Top Turret Gunner Haymon was unsuccessful in getting his turret to operate, but he managed to point the guns forward to give the impression they were in action. He then slipped out to aid the radio opeator, Sergeant Bewak, in moving the wounded copilot to the radio room.

Haymon took one look at the haggard Whitson. "Need some help?"

Whitson pointed weakly to the right seat. With his severe wounds, he had exhausted himself taking skillful evasive action throughout the attacks.

"How's the ammunition?" Whitson's voice shook as he turned to Haymon.

"We're nearly out at all stations," he said soberly.

With one prop feathered, they slipped into a heavy cloud formation and momentarily eluded the pursuing fighters.

Sergeant Meyer relieved Haymon at the controls as they emerged from the clouds.

Just then, Haymon yelled, "There's an ME-210 circling us. Watch him!"

The wounded bombardier crawled into the blasted, gaping nose to man the guns.

With the wind roaring like a hurricane through the shattered nose, Barrall fired burst after burst as the fighter closed in for the kill. The battered Fort refused to be an easy target, and Barrall fought off the fighter until it went into a steep dive with its port engine smoking heavily.

Barrall crawled out of the nose and up into the pilot's compartment. "Let me take over the controls," he said breathlessly. "You'll need to conserve your strength for the landing."

Sighting a formation off to their right, they joined it and headed for England.

Whitson took over the controls near the base although he was so weak from loss of blood he could hardly hold his head up. He shook his head occasionally to keep from passing out.

With no brakes or flaps to slow his speed, he landed at one hundred and fifty miles an hour and careened down the runway. Nearing the end, with his last remaining energy, he deftly ground-looped.

On the ground, anxious eyes had noted the flare from the plane during the approach so ambulances raced to the gallant airplane and its crew.

"That was a rugged mission, Curt," de Russy told LeMay that night.

The colonel glanced at the ceiling and sat back in his chair thoughtfully. "When you think what one formation went through without getting a bomb on the target." The operations officer opened his mouth to speak. LeMay cut him short. "I'm not blaming them. With a complete overcast, they had no choice but to jettison their bombs in the South Sea."

"The other formations did better," de Russy said. "They scored direct hits on the Heligoland Naval Base."

"This is one fifteenth of May that the participants will never forget," LeMay said. "All you have to do is study the crew reports to understand the ferocity of the attacks."

"They put up a good fight," de Russy said with pride. "Not one 305th aircraft was lost but they destroyed fifteen of the enemy."

"I see where the Germans are up to their old tricks of dropping bombs from above, trying to hit planes in the formation. It must be a frightening experience even though no damage is done."

Major Green walked in. "I have consistent reports," the intelligence officer said, "that the FDW-190's were painted to resemble P-47's and ME-109's were decorated to look like Spitfires."

LeMay's head snapped to attention. "Were the gunners fooled by this camouflage?"

"No," Green said with a grim smile. "They have fought too many duels with these airplanes to be taken in by a different paint job."

On the seventeenth of May, aircraft were dispatched to attack Lorient. During the bomb run and right through the flak at the target enemy fighters closed in with vigor. Unfortunately, the bombing was poor and three planes were lost to enemy action. A high toll was exacted from the Germans, who lost twelve fighters.

LeMay called in de Russy. His operations officer looked at him quizzically because the boss hadn't seemed himself the last few days.

"Call a meeting for tomorrow morning," LeMay said. "I've got something to tell all of you."

"Of course." He started to say something, thought better of it, and walked out.

• • •

A Day to Remember

The briefing room was crowded, and LeMay stood before them momentarily searching for words. There were so many familiar faces and so many memories of each of them. They quieted down, noting the somber aspect of his face.

"We've come a long way together," LeMay said huskily, "and now it's time for us to part."

They were so shocked at this disclosure they could hardly believe their ears.

"I have been ordered to take command of the 102nd Provisional Combat Wing," LeMay said.

They were stunned. A future without LeMay in command was unthinkable. They knew the job was a promotion, and deep inside they were proud he would soon become a general.

LeMay started to speak a couple of times, but all could see what a struggle was going on inside him. During training back in the States, they had thought him dour, cold, and too tough. They knew now he came closer to being a really great man than any commander they had known.

Finally, the words came haltingly and he thanked them in simple, eloquent phrases.

"My promotion," he said, "was earned not merely through my own efforts. It can be credited primarily to your sacrifices and unswerving devotion during the last year. Thank you very much."

The last words were almost muffled, and, to the astonishment of everyone present, their sturdy, black-haired, hazel-eyed boss was near the breaking point. He left hurriedly while the roof rang with a roar of approbation such as few men have ever heard.

The club was a scene of small groups, huddled together, discussing the unexpected turn of events.

With LeMay, if they had a new target, or a new mission involving new risks, they knew he would fly with them. They had complete confidence that if anyone could bring them through the roughest missions, he could.

In one group, McKee turned to Captain Adams. "I'd go to Hell and back for that man!"

Adams nodded vigorously. "Who wouldn't? He's never been much for words, but he's a determined man with a logical, analytical mind."

"There have been so many stories about him," McKeegan said reflectively. "The one I like best occurred on an early mission led by LeMay. The ball turret gunner called on the intercom to announce that his guns weren't working."

LeMay said, "You're gonna look pretty silly when those 190's start coming in!"

"Let me tell you," McKeegan said with a chuckle, "that turret was fixed in short order."

"We'll miss him," Adams said, "but he'll always be a part of us. His particular genius will be helping us over some of the rough spots. I hope he goes high in the Eighth Air force Command."

The next morning, LeMay called in Lieutenant Colonel Donald K. Fargo. "You're in command now. There's no finer group of men in the world. Take good care of them."

The slim Fargo stood straight and dignified before LeMay. "I'll do everything in my power, Curt, to carry on."

They shook hands, and LeMay hurried to his car. It

was a sad day for him as he was driven out the gate at Chelveston.

Such a wealth of memories flooded his consciousness that he knew his feelings towards these men could never be duplicated. He had been so much a part of them, and the memory of their sacrifices was so deeply embedded, they would hold first place in his heart and mind for the rest of his life.

CHAPTER 6

"I'll Fly Tail-End Charlie Too!"

FARGO HAD KNOWN it would not be easy to replace a man like LeMay, but he had gone about the task diligently and, after five weeks of the most bitter aerial warfare over the continent, he had endeared himself to the group.

The 305th's bombs had been aimed primarily at shipyards and dock areas at Wilhelmshaven and St. Nazaire during the last two weeks of May and the early part of June. The cities of Kiel and Bremen were attacked, but the most vicious air battle was fought over Kiel where the 305th lost four of its crews. The group's gunners claimed thirteen enemy aircraft destroyed.

Lieutenant Ralph McKee walked down the row of hospital beds to say good-bye to Sergeant Thomas J. McGrath. The wound in his back had healed since their plane had been severely damaged by flak over Lorient.

McGrath had fallen asleep, and McKee hesitated to awaken the painfully wounded ball turret gunner. It was still a mystery to him how any of them had come back alive. He knew it was due primarily to the cool-headedness of Captain Lyle Adams. Despite flak and fighters, and a battered B-17 that later had to be scrapped, Adams had continued on the bomb run and, through outstanding airmanship, had brought them back home.

McGrath must have sensed someone was near because he opened his eyes.

"Hi, Lieutenant," he said weakly. Noting McKee's full uniform, he said, "Getting out?"

He nodded. "They're sending me to the 'Flak Farm' for a week."

They both chuckled. The rest home, an old English castle near Southampton, was a standard joke among the crewmen who usually spent a week there midway in their combat tours.

"You don't look 'flakked up' to me," McGrath said with a smile.

"No," drawled McKee, "but I can use a few more days of rest and relaxation before going back to the group. How are you getting on?"

"Fine."

He looked at the strained face of the gunner, recalling with pride how he had stayed in his turret destroying several fighters after he had been hit twice in the stomach.

He and Sergeant Edison K. Danver in the tail turret had borne the brunt of the deadly fire. When they had arrived back at base both McGrath and Danver were more dead than alive.

When they shook hands, McGrath said, "I'll always remember Captain Adams singing 'Lonesome Cowboy' right in the thick of the flak and fighters, just as if he were sitting around a campfire back home. He's a cool one."

McKee looked at the gunner with admiration. "I won't ever forget how you fought, McGrath. You're as brave as they come."

The gunner's face flushed with embarrassment. "Oh, anyone would have done the same," he said modestly.

"Have you heard from your wife?" McKee said, glancing at the Catholic medal hanging around his neck.

"Yes," he said eagerly. "You know we were married just before we came over. I told her about being wounded. I kidded her that she must have let the candles go out that day."

"Good luck to you," McKee said. "Hope we'll see you back with the 305th soon."

"They'd better send me back there," McGrath said with determination. "I won't fly with any other outfit."

Fargo fingered his trim mustache as he studied the field order. His eyes opened wide as he saw it called for the first daylight mission into the Ruhr on June 22.

He knew what that meant! The Germans would resist their maximum effort to destroy the synthetic rubber plant at Huls, Germany, with everything they had.

"Sergeant," he called. "I want the squadron commanders in my office within fifteen minutes."

When McKee had reported back to the squadron from the "Flak Farm," he ran into "Roth" McKeegan. "You've had a rough time, Mac," McKeegan said. "Maybe the next mission will be an easy one so you can get back in the swing of things."

"None of them are easy," McKee said, feeling the familiar apprehension grip his insides.

Despite the efforts of the escorting Spitfire and Typhoon fighters who fought off a large number of enemy planes, the group had to fight their way in and fight their way out.

They were rewarded by a massive fire and billowing black smoke that rose to 20,000 feet, sufficient evidence they had placed a concentration of bombs near the aiming point.

The Blohm and Voss Shipyards at Hamburg were the target three days later as the Eighth Air Force continued to strike at German U-boat installations. Unfortunately, clouds obscured the area and a target of opportunity was bombed. One plane was lost as a result of attacks by one hundred and twenty-five enemy aircraft.

Three missions of minor significance followed with bombs falling on the airfield at Tricqueville, a lock at St. Nazaire and a mission abandoned en route to a German air base at Villacoublay.

McKee felt like a veteran as he prepared for his sixteenth mission on the Fourth of July. He had been named squadron navigator of the 366th the same time McKeegan was made operations officer.

Captain Adams and the enlisted men had completed their tours so he was assigned to another crew.

He turned to Bombardier Hank Wojdyla, who also had been assigned to the squadron staff. "There won't be a 'Lonesome Cowboy' along this time," he said. "I'll miss the old crew."

"It was a good one," Wojdyla said. "Keep your guns ready. There'll be some fireworks over Nantes today."

"I'll Fly Tail-End Charlie Too!"

* * *

Wojdyla stared unbelievingly as a sober-faced McKeegan described the raid after the crews returned.

"Wetzel's crew and McKee were shot down," he said hoarsely. "They were hit by flak on the bomb run and fell back behind the formation. There was nothing anyone could do," he said brokenly. "Three fighters worked them over and then two engines caught fire."

Wojdyla swallowed hard. "Did you spot any chutes?"

"All but two bailed out. Several reports indicate those in the forward section managed to escape."

They were too stunned to say more. Both had lost countless friends, but their crew had gone through so much together, the loss was a paralyzing one.

Throughout the month of July and the first two weeks of August 1943, the "Can Do" group concentrated on a program to destroy the German Air Force at its bases. When weather permitted, they struck deeper and deeper into Germany to bomb its industrial cities.

Cities receiving the greatest tonnage of bombs included Kassel, Kiel, and Gelsenkirchen. One extremely long mission took them to Heroya, Norway, a new direction for the group at extreme range from their base.

When the crews returned August 16 after bombing the airfield at Le Bourget where Lindbergh landed after his memorable journey across the Atlantic, they were unanimous in saying, "We sure plastered it! That was the best bombing we've seen."

The next mission began in the usual way, but only the beginning was usual. At 10 P.M. that evening, a teletype order was rushed to Fargo's office.

His face flushed with excitement as he tore open the

envelope and started to read. He saw quickly that it implemented the long-anticipated strike which was part of a greater plan of the 8th Bomber Command aimed at destruction of the German ball-bearing plants at Schweinfurt and Regensburg.

Fargo picked up the telephone and quickly placed calls to the various sections.

The base was in a fever of excitement as the armament officer translated the list of items on his "frag" into the more meaningful terms of types of bombs and ammunition. The communications' officer went to work on the complicated frequencies and times of operation of the various navigational aids. His task was a difficult one because no radio beacon stayed on the same frequency, or used the same call sign, or broadcast from the same site for more than three minutes at a time. To do so, was almost certain death.

The beacons, a most important part of each navigator's kit of tools, were switched on and off, varied in frequency, broadcast from different stations, and sounded by different call signs in a meticulously planned "random" manner.

All of the frequencies, locations, call signs, and times were printed on rice paper impregnated with sugar. Navigators and radio operators varied in their comments whether or not this was a tasty tidbit in the event the secret information had to be chewed up.

The flight line was a beehive of activity as the Flying Fortresses were carefully prepared for the dangerous mission, and tough crew chiefs threatened dire things if the younger mechanics took their jobs too casually.

Group specialists worked throughout the night to prepare the kits of maps, charts, pictures, and briefing ma-

"I'll Fly Tail-End Charlie Too!"

terial so vital to the success of the mission.

The duty navigator was oblivious of everything as he performed a most important service. Alone, bending over a plotting board, he took the required time and place of departure from England and worked backwards along the flight route. Figuring in the twenty-two minutes it would take the group to take off and form in combat formation, he subtracted two hours for briefing, two more for arising, messing, and gathering, and gave the operations officer the time the crews should be awakened.

The crews were unaware of what was taking place on the official side of the base. In the club, a loud argument was underway in a corner occupied by several officers of the 366th Squadron.

After a while, much of the usual banter had been used up and a discussion arose about combat missions—tough ones, milk runs.

Lieutenant Robert E. Wirt, a navigator in the squadron, was philosophical. "We've flown some that can be called tough ones," he said. "There've been a few definite milk runs, but those in between can best be classified according to each crew's personal experience."

There were various blunt shades of opinion from the others, but, in general, they were in agreement.

"You can always count on a rough one," Wirt said, "when you tangle with the Messerschmitts with the checkerboard noses protecting the Hamburg-Kiel area. They're real rough on the low squadrons."

"Don't forget the 'Abbeville Kids,'" a pilot said. "Those yellow-nosed Focke-Wulfes are masters at frontal attacks."

"The flak at St. Nazaire is deadly to the lead squadrons," Wirt said. "We nicknamed that place 'flak city' with good reason."

It was getting close to an early club-closing time, so they started to drift away. A pilot winked at the others and turned to Roth McKeegan, operations officer for the squadron.

"All I can say," he said loudly, "I ought to be an operations officer. Then I'd take nothing but the easy ones. Operations officers get to pick their own missions—and they only pick the milk runs."

A sudden quiet followed his remarks. All eyes fastened on McKeegan, and the indomitable spirit of a fighting Irishman rose in righteous indignation. He climbed on top of his chair and, with a face brick-red with anger, roared, "Pick my missions?" He had to pause momentarily to control himself. "I don't pick my missions! Just for that I'll schedule myself for the very next mission." He had worked himself up into such a state that he had to pause again for breath. "And I'll fly tail-end Charlie *too!*"

Somehow, what had been said in jest, lost its appeal. They suddenly were reminded of the deadly game they were playing. Their faces became serious and lost youthfulness as they left the club singly without another word.

CHAPTER 7

A Trail of Burning Fortresses

THE MISSION WAS the most secretively planned the group had been engaged in, but it also was the first in which the target was known to a great number of airmen before the attack.

This paradox can be explained by the vital importance of the target and the fact that General LeMay's new 3rd Air Divisioin would overfly the Alps and land at North African bases.

The navigators and bombardiers had been briefed ahead of time on special maps from which all references had been removed. It was vitally important for them to identify the target so no errors would develop.

The complex of rivers, roads, railroads, mountains, and other landmarks in the target area led unerringly to the location of Schweinfurt on a normal planning chart.

The name of the 305th's target had been a familiar

item of conversation in the officers' barracks as the expected mission had been called up, scrubbed as the B-17's sat on the runway waiting for the green light, called up again, scrubbed again until now, on the morning of August 17, the men joked about another scrub for Schweinfurt. They joked in the manner of men who knew that if it did come off, it would be no joking matter!

The crews listened thoughtfully to the briefing. Their serious faces reflected concern, but Fargo could tell that inwardly they were glad the mounting suspense and the endless rumors were at an end.

"Do you have anything to add?" the intelligence officer said to the colonel.

His grave face matched the mood of the hundreds of crew members as he stood up.

"Today's mission to Schweinfurt is a maximum effort. Every B-17 in commission has been assigned. Instead of the usual 75 per cent, we have set up 100 per cent of the airplanes. I emphasize this point to stress the importance of the target. The 1st Air Division, of which we are a part, has five combat wings totaling more than 300 Flying Fortresses. We have added one B-17 to each squadron, right down to the bottom to keep tail-end Charlie company. This means each group has twenty-one aircraft and each combat wing sixty-three B-17's.

"The three regular combat wings will be joined in the division formation by a wing composed of the extra groups and by a 'Composite Wing.' This has been formed from the various leftovers of the combat wings and groups."

Fargo searched his mind for the right words to spur them to do their utmost, but a glance at their serious faces convinced him that further words were useless.

A Trail of Burning Fortresses

On the flight line, the maintenance crews made their final checks with a solemnity characteristic of their intense devotion. These were their B-17's because the Flying Fortresses really belonged to the men who kept them flying and not the here-today-gone-tomorrow air crews.

Armorers had loaded boxes of fifty-caliber bullets while the armament experts filled the bomb bays with a strange assortment of bright colored bombs. Air crews looking up into the bays thought they looked like something out of Buck Rogers. The stubby, efficient 500 pounders had been replaced with long, tapered shapes with graceful tail fins. These were not high-explosive but British fire bombs.

At take-off time, heavy fog shrouded Chelveston. The ceiling-zero conditions with visibility ranging from fifty to one hundred yards, merely added to Major Price's forebodings about the deep penetration into the Reich.

The new squadron commander of the 422nd Squadron climbed aboard Lieutenant Cramer's aircraft to lead a composite group of the 305th and 306th.

The sureness of their preparations relieved his mind momentarily. They were an experienced lead crew, and he was glad to have capable hands over such a target. He knew the mission was an open invitation to the Luftwaffe. He had no illusions whatsoever about the hours ahead of them.

"Are we really ready to go this time?" Cramer said.

"The delays are over," Price said. "This time it's for real."

Several exasperating delays had been authorized by Bomber Command because of the weather, so final take-off was three and a half hours later than originally planned.

This increase in the time interval between the Regensburg and Schweinfurt formations was to have an important effect on the opposition encountered over Germany and the losses sustained by the 1st Wing.

"The clouds have broken up a bit," Cramer said anxiously, as he taxied to the end of the runway. "Wish this fog would lift a few feet."

At 11:40 A.M. Cramer lifted his Fortress off the runway and they climbed through fog and clouds. At thirty second intervals, twenty-eight more followed, although one aircraft had to return because of faulty oxygen systems.

"We should have good support from the P-47 Thunderbolts," Price said. "A lot of water has passed through the Channel since the days when they sat up at thirty thousand feet and dared the Focke-Wulfes to do battle with them. They're supposed to stay close to the formation."

They crossed the coast of England, and Cramer mentally noted this was zero hour. Now, he knew, everything that had been played in a minor key would be played in the major.

As the combat wings of the 1st Air Division passed Splasher Seven, a beacon on the coast of East Saxony, the five combat wings were formed in the familiar high-on-the-right, low-on-the-left formation which made each combat wing look from the front or rear like a long diagonal line and, from any other view, like a flight of geese.

Two regular wings led off the parade with the 101st Combat Wing, the successor to the old 1st Combat Wing which had, in the spring of 1943, been the Eighth Air Force, in the second position followed by the composite

A Trail of Burning Fortresses

wing. The odd-group wing and another regular wing brought up the rear.

The 305th occupied the low position in the wing, with the 366th Squadron in the low position of the group, and, bringing up the rear and "filling in the diamond," the lowest and most vulnerable of the sixty-three heavily loaded Flying Fortresses was "Smilin' Thru," a B-17, named after an old Irish ballad and flown by a young Irish pilot, First Lieutenant Rothery McKeegan.

Price knew this was to be one of the deepest penetrations into German territory ever made by American bombers, traversing more of the most heavily defended territory than any other.

Unlike the missions to the northern submarine yards and aircraft factories, where long hours of over-water flight allowed a more leisurely climb to bombing altitude, all of the twenty-four thousand feet of this mission was climbed in a wide circle.

Price watched the Thunderbolts with admiration. With a perfection of timing that would do credit to the Radio City Rockettes, dozens of them, with their white noses and elliptical wings flashing in the sun, laced back and forth a few hundred feet above the top Forts.

The flight across France was uneventful. "No 'Abbeville Kids,'" Price said thankfully.

Cramer nodded. "The P-47's are a comforting sight."

They both watched as the fighters lazily slid in and out, lifting a wing as if to say, "Don't shoot! I'm your friend."

The relaxing effect of the P-47's was something no one had foreseen, but the Luftwaffe took full advantage of it. While B-17 gunners were leaning on their guns watching the friendly fighters slide in, tip a wing, and slide out again, the first of the formations reached the Rhine River south of Frankfurt.

A startled gunner, the first to notice the fighter wing tipped up before his eyes wasn't round—but square!—was shocked to find the air filled with tracers.

"Price to crew. Those white-nosed airplanes are Focke-Wulfes. The 'Abbeville Kids' are in disguise again today. Let 'em have it."

Price's face was set in grim lines. Ahead of him flaming Fortresses were falling in such numbers that he lost count. "Our navigator has an easy job today," he said without humor. "All he has to do is follow the trail of burning Fortresses and parachutes from the task forces ahead of us."

Cramer nodded. "They're attacking in groups of fourteen now," he said tensely.

Twin-engine fighters stood out of range and fired broadsides. ME-109's fired rockets, and they burst around them without seeming to do any damage.

The stragglers, who had been damaged, were having a particularly bad time. Attacks were made by groups of fighters from two directions on the tail.

Over Flushing, ten black bursts of anti-aircraft fire surrounded them at twenty-two thousand five hundred feet.

Northeast of Antwerp, flak again burst in black and white colors near them.

Two green bursts appeared near the formation. "I wonder what that signifies?" Cramer said anxiously.

"A signal," Price said. Enemy fighters poured a hail of bullets at them.

Flak followed them relentlessly during the rest of the flight to the target, but the fighters left them relatively

A Trail of Burning Fortresses

alone and concentrated on the formations at the target.

Price noted one B-17 at seventeen thousand feet surrounded by four Nazi fighters. It didn't have a chance. It headed earthward in a steep dive and exploded with a blinding flash upon contact with the ground.

Seven miles northeast of Louvain, a B-17 exploded on the ground. "Six got out," Cramer said tensely. He pointed to the chutes floating below them.

At 2:51, a B-17 tumbled out of the sky and eight bodies hurtled grotesquely from the flaming bomber and their chutes snapped open.

The group ahead was fighting desperately. One of their B-17's began to smoke, and only four crewmen managed to exit the doomed bomber.

Lieutenant Norman Bennett could see the smoking target where it had been severely mauled by the preceding formations. While he hastily made his adjustments on the sight, he saw eight parachutes in the air below him while a B-17 fluttered awkwardly to earth out of control.

At 3:05, his bombs went away and plunged towards the target twenty-two thousand two hundred feet beneath him. The flak was heavy and he noticed the group ahead was taking the full brunt of it.

Then it was their turn and a black barrage surrounded them as the shrapnel slammed into the aircraft. He glanced briefly at the ground and noted with satisfaction that his bombs chewed their way through the heart of the factory. Then he grabbed his nose guns.

Fighter attacks came in waves as they turned away from the target and headed anxiously for England.

The bombardier watched, in horrified fascination, as a B-17, at ten thousand feet, headed down with two engines aflame and five fighters hot on its tail. He swallowed tightly as the plane hit the ground with a blinding flash.

South of St. Trond, a bomber with its number four engine on fire was tailed by an FW-190. It continued to return the Nazi's fire but it went down steadily, and only three crewmen bailed out.

"Watch 564!" Price called. "That's one of ours."

Flames covered the wing. Exit doors flew off, but only five chutes appeared.

At the bottom of the tightly knit 101st Wing, McKeegan struggled to maintain control of his B-17 after two engines had been shot out. He advanced the power of the two remaining engines to hold the 160 mile an hour speed of the rest of the wing.

The leader, seeing his predicament, slowed the formation to 150 miles an hour. This gave only a brief respite to the valiant efforts of "Smilin' Thru" and its crew.

Finally, the composite wing, with no more than twenty Forts in helter-skelter formation, broke up as individual planes dashed for the relative safety of the other wings.

Price watched a Fort at sixteen thousand feet circling down with smoke pouring from it and enemy fighters hot on its tail. Suddenly, as his throat constricted, the B-17 blew up. Eight men tumbled out of the bomber in an incredible escape, although one parachute was on fire and the body of the helpless man dropped sickeningly to the ground.

On the route back to Frankfurt, the Luftwaffe tried a new weapon. As crews of the B-17's watched Messerschmitt 210's fly alongside a thousand yards away, making no apparent effort to get ahead and start a fighter pass, they were puzzled at first. Suddenly, at the wing

A Trail of Burning Fortresses 87

roots of the enemy fighters, a bright red flare blossomed, becoming larger and larger until a huge blast went off in the B-17 formation.

They were chilled to the marrow by the attacks of crude rockets although they did no damage. Unnoticed by the crews, a German plane overhead told the rocket-carrying fighters when to fire.

When the 101st Wing passed south of Frankfurt once more, a Messerschmitt 110, the tried and true two-seater of the Luftwaffe, led two rocket-bearing ME-210's in a classic pursuit curve from the left and level with the formation. As the 110, leading the way, entered the center of his turn, outlining the twin-engined pattern of his plane in the afternoon sun, a friendly P-47 darted from above, striking the Messerschmitt with the full force of its heavy guns, and the 110 flew to pieces. Flaming engines fell separately, pieces of wing and fuselage fluttered crazily in the air, and the 305th flew through it.

Pieces of the Messerschmitt hit several 305th airplanes with negligible damage except for McKeegan's Flying Fortress which, despite two engines out, desperately hung on to the formation.

Major Price's eyes were scalded by tears as he saw "Smilin' Thru" roll over and begin to spew out parachutes. His face quivered with emotion as the veteran of many a 305th mission began its descent to become another of the many smoking hulks of aircraft which marked the passage of the formation as far as eyes could see back into the eastern mountains.

The return of the American Thunderbolts, who had picked up the Forts at the limit of their own range, marked the end of the battle. Ironically, it was this symbol of safety the entire division had been seeking that placed the coup de grace on the desperate efforts of "Roth" McKeegan who, as operations' officer, could pick his own missions—and did!

Simultaneously, another squadron plane was stricken although a P-47 tried to fight off the 190 without success. The B-17 tore itself apart from the punishment, and eight men hastily bailed out.

Price had counted at least eighteen B-17's going down during the route back. Some had exploded in mid-air and no parachutes appeared. Others, with part of the wing shot away, or the tail chopped off by the savagery of the 20 mm. cannon attacks, had cart wheeled out of the sky and burst with shattering crashes on the populated countryside below them.

He was appalled by the sight, but they grimly held their heading and hoped for the best. He figured roughly they had encountered at least one hundred and fifty enemy fighters. He was surprised by the different types. He had seen ME-109's, ME-110's, FW-190's and, much to his astonishment, the old dive bomber, the JU-88.

Finally, they were over the Channel and they breathed sighs of relief. Many aircraft, because the mission's distance had been the maximum they could fly, were forced to land at the English Coast to refuel.

Colonel Fargo read the congratulatory wire from Brigadier General Robert B. Williams, commander of the wing. Despite sheer exhaustion, Fargo felt a warmth within him as he read the words of praise for the successful accomplishment of the mission.

He knew the target had received severe damage even though the bombing had not been perfect. The experienced leaders, despite the ferocity of the enemy attacks, kept their formations and withstood the mightiest display of enemy attacks they had as yet received.

Fargo was astonished by the tremendous number of claims. In noting the group had fought off enemy fighters for an hour and eighteen minutes to the target, and another hour and seven minutes in return, he noted with pride that the gunners had been credited with destroying seventeen fighters.

After the interrogation, Cramer turned to Price. "Major, there's no point in returning to that target. No more ball bearings will be produced there for a long time."

"I hope you're right," Price said thoughtfully. "Don't count on it. I've seen the photographs and I wouldn't be surprised if it will need another pummeling."

"Oh no, sir!" Cramer said in shocked tones.

Price nodded soberly and slowly walked away.

The 305th had exacted a toll, but they also paid a price with two aircraft shot down by enemy fighters.

The wing had sent a total of two hundred and thirty aircraft, and one hundred and eighty-three had bombed the primary target.

Eighth Air Force losses were heavy, with thirty-six aircraft failing to return. Of this number, twenty-six were shot down by fighters, one was destroyed by flak, and nine did not return for unknown causes.

Fargo was aware of a noticeable sag in combat morale after the mission. For one thing, the crews had expected extra liberty privileges after maintaining a long period of alert. The necessity of continuing the offensive after the Germans had shot down over one hundred Allied heavy bombers over Germany on this mission and others during the preceding twenty-four hours was explained to them. Fargo did his best, but he could not make an impression on the exhausted crews.

He knew they had been told the Royal Air Force would follow the raid with a maximum effort. He couldn't tell them, however, that through no fault of the R.A.F., this was impossible because of adverse weather conditions. He could not explain this to the crews at the time because of tight security, so they felt they had been let down after their bloody fight to pave the way.

In discussing their problems with the group commanders, General Williams noted with extreme regret that his newly designated 1st Division had been so decimated by losses during the week that he had only six combat group formations available for strikes until suitable replacements came in.

The group commanders sympathized with their general. They, too, were appalled by the heavy losses, regardless of how much they appreciated the necessity for continuing operations.

CHAPTER 8

"The Target Must Be Destroyed!"

BY NOW THE 305th was well acquainted with the possibilities inherent in its type of warfare and deeper penetrations were possible. Accustomed to enemy air opposition and flak defenses, the group knew what to expect and how to handle it. For a while, and much to their relief, the attacks continued against airfields in France close to home.

During September and the early part of October, strikes against the enemy's air power continued but German industrial targets at Bremen and Stuttgart also were bombed.

For some time, the Eighth Air Force had recognized the need for greater range in the B-17. Engineers worked night and day to develop full-length fuel tanks in the wing. Appearing first in the B-17G's, these powerful new aircraft also were equipped with vitally needed chin turrets.

After they became available and the earlier models of the B-17F were modified at Burtonwood, the planners looked for targets beyond their previous ranges.

On October 9, Lieutenant Robert E. Wirt, recently promoted to group navigator, watched the faces of the crew members as they settled down for the briefing.

From their comments, he knew they expected another short mission. When the curtains were drawn from the route map at the front of the room, gasps and whistles went up as the operations officer set up an extension to the right of the regular wall map.

Although he had been in on the intense planning for the mission, when he saw the long red tape stretch across the enlarged chart his feelings were tinged with disbelief. His eyes followed the tape, paused momentarily at their former limit, then moved on, twice as far as the group had ever gone before, until it finally stopped at the bay of Danzig.

Feeling a light hand on his shoulder, he turned to look into the eager eyes of Lieutenant Henry F. Wojdyla.

"I've waited a long time," the group bombardier said quietly. His eyes were kindled with intense emotion. "Just get me within sight of the place, and I'll do the rest."

They had flown so many times as a team that Wirt knew exactly how he felt. It occurred to him that Hank's opportunity to strike at the German shipyards at Gdynia, where the Germans had sent the remnants of their high-seas fleet including the Schleswig-Holstein, was poetic justice. For it was this ancient battle cruiser that had opened World War II by firing on the Polish Naval Acad-

"The Target Must Be Destroyed!"

emy at Gdynia. The guns manned by the brave Polis naval cadets were no match for the massive firepower of the big ship. They would soon see, Wirt thought grimly, how good the German gunners were now against an experienced Polish hand at the controls of a Norden bombsight and a fleet of Flying Fortresses.

Wirt looked at him with admiration while Hank lit up a cigar. He already had proved his artistry on the synthetic oil factory at Huls, the synthetic rubber factory at Hanover, and the oil factory at Gelsenkirchen, among others.

He knew Wojdyla had received the rewards for his outstanding work, but Wirt felt in his heart that it was men like Hank who had proved that the theory of precision bombing was not only practical but the most sensible way to obtain results.

The briefing started, but Wirt's thoughts were elsewhere. He and Hank had spent so many hours planning it; the specialist reports were too familiar. His mind went over their plans again.

During their many missions together, they had developed a system all their own. In effect, it was a two-navigator system with another man in a specially equipped compartment near the radioman.

This permitted him and Hank to lead the formations expertly to the target. Wirt navigated strictly by pilotage, rarely taking his eyes from the ground, but following the course from each road crossing to woodland, from each stream bend to village square and on to the initial point.

Near the target, they compared observations as Wirt looked directly at the ground and Hank looked through his instrument. Once their views coincided, the bombardier tracked ahead until they had assured themselves he was on the aiming point.

94 The Incredible 305th

It was a good system, Wirt thought, one in which two heads proved better than one. He knew, however, that after Hank was lined up with the aiming point, it was up to him to pinpoint the bombs.

Fargo took a long draw on his cigarette, crushed it out in a can, and mounted the platform. "This is the first full-range mission for the 305th," he said. "A total of four hundred B-17's and B-24's, by far the largest force yet assembled, will participate.

"Other wings will attack the shipyards at Danzig, the aircraft factories at Marienburg while several wings will turn off past Kiel as a diversion. They will penetrate to the south to attack targets at Anklam." He stood slim and straight for a moment. And then, as if he realized any kind of pep talk was out of place for such men, he merely said, "Good luck!"

Wirt held his pilotage map before him as his eyes moved first to the ground and then back to the map. They were flying at only a thousand feet as they headed for Splasher Five, a radio beacon at Cromer.

Wirt noticed the Lancasters of the R.A.F. returning from a night strike. As they passed, each one raised his wing in greeting. It was an inspiring sight, and he felt a thrill of recognition for their comrades-in-arms.

From Cromer, they climbed at a steady one hundred feet per minute, on a course to keep them north of the Frisian Islands and their giant Wurzburg radars.

"I hope our low altitude and the distance from the radar sets will help us to sneak through," Wirt said to Hank.

"So do I," he said. "If we can get to the Danish

Peninsula without their knowing it, we'll enjoy an element of surprise."

Approaching the coast of Denmark, Wirt altered course to take the formation south of Copenhagen.

"Don't forget the coastal flak batteries," Hand said anxiously.

"I won't." He gave the pilot another slight change of course, and the wing went into a gentle skidding turn as they crossed the coast.

They looked at one another with satisfaction. Not a gun had fired at them.

Continuing on to the Kattegat, the Anklam force increased its rate of climb and turned south to enter Germany east of Berlin.

The wing droned on across the Baltic Sea, gaining altitude with every mile, flying south of the Swedish Island of Bornholm, and then penetrating the north coast of Germany east of Peenemünde.

"The Danzig and Marienburg wings are leaving us," Wojdyla said.

Flak appeared as they neared the initial point at Gdynia.

A red-red flare erupted from the lead Flying Fortress, and the low group peeled off to make its run.

The two members of the team hunched over the bombsight as they flew for thirty seconds and then made a slow turn to the left.

Wojdyla was in a high state of excitement as the two worked together to get the formation lined up with the target.

The bombardier, who had been peering intently through the telescope, looked at Wirt with consternation. "The harbor is obscured by a dense cover of smoke."

Wirt had seen the smoke pouring from pots along the shore and continuing downwind to cover the harbor.

"Bombardier to pilot! I can't see the aiming point from this heading. We're making a second run."

Although the pilot had severe qualms, he clicked the intercom and remained silent while he was given the new heading.

Wirt directed the group into a sharp turn to obtain room to make a run from the south parallel to the coast.

"The other groups didn't get the word," Wojdyla said desperately. "Look at them!"

They watched the low group draw quickly away while the high group slid above them intent on their scheduled run.

As they turned up the coast, they could see the other wings bombing at Danzig, with their bombs falling into the smoke.

After trying a new heading, the bombardier said, "I've got to have another heading! I won't bomb blindly!"

By now, the flak, while not severe, was finding them accurately but fighters failed to materialize.

Although the entire group viewed a third run with apprehension, they did not question his command. They all were as excited as he was with the emotional drama.

Wirt quickly saw that the only place Hank could hope to see anything was at the source of the smoke, in the area where the billowing clouds had not yet merged to cover the area.

He called the pilot and gave him a new heading, directing the group to be turned to the east.

The 305th flew upwind out over the bay of Danzig.

Wojdyla looked up at Wirt with mounting excitement.

"The Target Must Be Destroyed!"

"I can catch glimpses of steel-gray shapes in the smoke."

Wirt watched him anxiously as he started his run, and, peering at the ground, he saw that it was the Germans themselves who gave him his aiming point. Relying on the smoke to hide them from the down-wind approaches, they had abandoned this defense when they saw the 305th come in from the north. Wirt watched the bombardier intently as his hands played delicately with the knobs of the bombsight.

"Bombs away!" he yelled.

Smoke covered the harbor basin so neither could tell how well the bombs had been aimed.

They faced a situation now that none of the 305th had anticipated. At twenty thousand feet over the Polish Corridor, with all the other groups out of sight ahead of them, the eighteen Fortresses of the 305th took off in a straight line for a point south of Copenhagen.

"Pilot to crew. The oxygen line has been ruptured. Only an emergency supply remains. Use it sparingly."

They sat as still as possible, and kept movement within the aircraft to a minimum to conserve the precious oxygen.

In crossing the Swedish Island of Bornholm again, four salvos of flak were fired with precision. One burst behind them, another to their left, one to the right, and the last five hundred yards straight ahead—precisely on their flight altitude.

Wirt chuckled to himself. The Swedes had made it so obvious. They had maintained the integrity of their homeland, but it was more of a salute than guns fired in anger.

While the men in the lead Fortress gasped the last of their oxygen and the group descended to a lower altitude, they noticed ahead hundreds of B-17's and B-24's, combat wings of all types in good formations, but without a semblance of the long line of eight combat wings which had left Cromer so many hours before.

All the way across the North Sea, the groups of bombers gradually moved into battle-line formation which strung for miles. The Anklam force, badly battered but happy to be back with friends, joined them as they headed for England.

With the sun disappearing in the west, ten and a half hours after they had departed the Midlands, they were greeted by the red and green wing-tip lights of countless Lancasters dipping in salute as their friends of the morning hurried eastward for another bombing of Germany.

After the final de-briefing, a very tired lead crew, still breathing a bit deeper than normal, hit the sack.

It was not known until the reports of the R.A.F. Mosquito reconnaissance mission were received the following day that the larger part of the German fleet rested on the bottom of the bay. Among them was the Schleswig-Holstein which Wojdyla's bombs had sent to the bottom beneath the guns of the Polish Naval Academy!

A good pattern of bombs was dropped on the railroad tracks and warehouses in the town of Enschede, Holland, the next day. It was attacked after the group was forced off its bombing run at Münster to avoid colliding with another formation.

When Lieutenant Ralph McKee reported back to the group after his escape from France, he was the object of much attention from the old-timers.

In operations, he described what had happened to the crew after the July 4 raid.

"Bill Wetzel and I met at a Frenchman's house," he said, "after we bailed out at 22,000 feet. For the next six weeks, we evaded capture while we headed for the Spanish border. The Spaniards interned us for two weeks but let us leave for England."

"What happened to the rest of the crew?" a pilot said.

"We heard later that six of them were captured the same day we were shot down. They probably ended up in Stalag III."

McKee celebrated his promotion to captain September 27, eight days after his twenty-second birthday.

Shortly thereafter, he received orders for rotation home.

In saying good-bye to the few intimates who remained with the group, "I feel thirty-five years old," he said wearily. "When I think back what these men have accomplished, it hardly seems possible. Most of the men we came over with are gone," he said sadly.

At the end of the briefing October 14, Fargo stood up and faced the eighteen crews who were scheduled for the second Schweinfurt mission. He could see in their faces that they were appalled by the prospect of a return to the dreaded target. They sat solemnly in front of him as he started to speak.

"The operation today is the most important yet conducted in this war. The target must be destroyed! It is of vital importance to the enemy. Your friends and comrades who have been lost, and who will be lost today, are depending on you. Their sacrifices must not have been in vain. Good luck, good shooting, and good bombing!"

Major G.G.Y. Normand, commanding officer of the 365th Squadron, muttered, "We'll need the good luck part of it."

After take-off, three aircraft were forced to cancel the mission because of mechanical difficulties.

Normand surveyed the fifteen ship formation with grave misgivings. They would need all the massed firepower they could spare, and the early loss of three aircraft could be crucial.

The importance of the target, and its value to the German economy, was much in his mind as they formed closely together after their P-47 escort departed at 1:33 P.M.

Three forces of seven combat wings had been alerted to strike against the three main and subsidiary factories manufacturing ball and roller bearings. The first two forces were to have B-17 aircraft of the 1st and 3rd Bombardment Divisions totaling six combat wings of sixty aircraft each. The plan called for the third force to have one combat wing of sixty B-24 aircraft from the 2nd Bombardment Division to attack thirty minutes after the previous two forces had bombed.

The strategy of the attack called for the first two forces to penetrate the enemy defenses in line abreast, some thirty miles apart, as far as the range of their fighter escort.

The following force was to fly a longer route to the south so a suitable bombing interval would occur prior to reaching the target area. This was planned in the belief that the enemy fighter forces would be exhausted from their encounters with the preceding forces.

All three forces were scheduled for a southerly course on their return so enemy aircraft would have difficulty

"The Target Must Be Destroyed!"

in maintaining active contact with the formations. Nazi fighter planes, limited by fuel capacities, had a relatively small radius of action. This southerly route on return was more desirable from a weather viewpoint as low stratus clouds were forecast with low ceilings and low visibility beneath them.

Actually, smaller numbers were dispatched on the mission than the plan called for and the third force aborted.

Inasmuch as the route was beyond the maximum range of the normal endurance of the B-17, aircraft not equipped with special fuel tanks carried a bomb bay tank.

Each force had been assigned a group of American P-47's on penetration for maximum range, another group for withdrawal, and also four squadrons of English Spitfires for withdrawal.

In addition, one group of two Spitfire squadrons was to sweep the area of withdrawal five minutes after the last force crossed the enemy beltline defenses, particularly as defense for stragglers.

Major Normand watched the fighter escort as they dipped their wings in salute and headed home.

"Enemy fighters! Eight o'clock, high!"

His mind was jarred roughly back to reality.

Singly, and in groups in three, four, and five, the fighters came at them. All types of fighters struck viciously at the formation.

Normand was appalled by the massed waves of attackers, and the intercom was silent—voices would have been drowned out by the thunderous roar of the aircraft's guns.

The 305th staggered through the holocaust, and Normand's hands trembled as one by one B-17's of the group broke apart and headed earthward. The sky was full of parachutes and blazing bombers. It seemed impossible any of them could get through to the target.

The attacks proceeded unrelentingly as they approached the target with another formation.

"Let's make a separate run," the bombardier called.

"Stay with the formation!" Normand said quickly. His last glance at his own formation wisely decided him not to leave the protection of the group in front of them. He knew something the bombardier did not—there were only two other planes left in the 305th!

The bombs went away slightly to the left of the aiming point towards the center of Schweinfurt.

Normand's bloodshot eyes stared unbelievingly as another B-17 exploded right before his eyes, and now there were only two battered Fortresses of the gallant band of men who had left Chelveston that morning.

At 4:47 P.M., the fighter attacks finally ended.

Anxious ground crews in England peered into the dusk in the east until the sound of engines was heard. They looked at one another in consternation as only two B-17's came in for landings.

It was some comfort that night for the group to receive a teletype message from Eighth Air Force Headquarters.

"A conservative estimate of the results of the attack," it said, "places the loss at seventy-five per cent of the productive capacity of the ball-bearing industry at Schweinfurt."

They were too stunned by the tragedy to recover for some time. They just prayed they would not have to return.

Fargo noted that the raid had seen familiar German tactics, but never had so many fighters rose to oppose them. Four hundred fighters of all types had challenged their passage, and Fargo grimly told the staff, "Although the cost was staggering, the men chose death rather than turn back!"

The intelligence officers learned during the critique that single-engine fighters came in waves, firing large numbers of rockets from projectors beneath their wings.

All formations reported the rockets lobbing towards them from a thousand-yard range sought out the lead elements.

The 40th Combat Wing, spearheading the attack of the 1st Division, lost twenty-nine of its forty-nine airplanes.

Despite its devastating losses, the 40th had placed 53 per cent of its bombs within one thousand feet of the aiming point.

The two hundred and twenty-eight B-17's that succeeded in bombing dropped three hundred and ninety-five tons of high explosives and eighty-eight tons of incendiaries on all three of the big bearing plants.

Germany had to reorganize its bearing industry following this strategic attack on Schweinfurt, but the bomber loss was almost crippling. Of all who went on the mission, sixty crews failed to return.

Fargo reported the final evaluation to the staff. "This strike caused the most damage and the greatest interference with production," he said. "German industrial planners are so alarmed they have taken a grave view of future attacks."

Machine damage amounted to only 10 per cent although Allied interpreters at the time thought over 50 per cent of Germany's capacity for producing bearings had been destroyed.

The damage had an impact, however, in important segments of the industry. If the attacks could have been continued, a critical bearing situation would have developed.

The Eighth Air Force had good reasons for failing to return to Schweinfurt for more than four months. By this time, the Germans had reorganized the industry in a more protected manner so it was impossible to destroy. The bomber loss on the first big raid had been so severe that additional deep penetrations without fighter escort were considered impossible. New Allied fighters, designed with a capability for longer range of operations, were then only in the development stage.

Gunners claimed one hundred and eighty-six fighters, but postwar analysis scaled this down to thirty-eight fighters destroyed in combat and twenty damaged. An additional five fighters lost on that date, according to German records, undoubtedly belong to these totals.

LeMay, now commander of the 3rd Bombardment Division, said bluntly, "All crews again have been impressed with the importance of making every possible effort to complete the destruction of each target on the first attempt thus making it unnecessary to return later."

During this week of many costly air battles, the Air Force had lost one hundred and forty-eight bombers and crews in air actions over the continent.

Fighter escort to and from the target was paramount for all deep penetrations into the Reich, but such full support was still in the future. Meanwhile, the 305th still had a job to do.

CHAPTER 9

Distinguished Unit Citation

ALTHOUGH THE GROUP had not recovered from the shock of Schweinfurt, within five days they were back over Germany striking at industrial targets.

Fargo relinquished group leadership during the early part of the month to Colonel Delmar Wilson, a tall, dark-haired officer with a distinguished background in the bombardment field.

During a raid November 26 against Bremen, continuous fighter attacks developed just before the IP until the coast was crossed on the way out an hour later.

The aircraft in which Sergeant Marcus A. Boudreaux was flying was attacked by enemy fighters who bored in from the nose and tail. In the ensuing battle, he was thrown from his gun position and his left eye blinded by an exploding cannon shell. Despite the pain of his wound, Boudreaux returned immediately to his guns and fought off repeated enemy attacks. Shortly thereafter, he was wounded again by a shell from an attacking enemy fighter. Although he was suffering intensely from shock and wounds, he continued to fight until the attacks subsided.

The explosion had damaged the oxygen system, and, after the attacks ceased, he searched frantically for a walk-around bottle since he was rapidly losing strength from lack of oxygen and loss of blood.

Upon entering the waist compartment, he saw the ball turret gunner trying to leave his shattered turret. Almost unconscious from lack of oxygen, Boudreaux disregarded his own condition and immediately went to his aid. Meanwhile, enemy planes attacked again so Boudreaux hastily returned to his guns.

About thirty-five hundred feet above the group formation enemy bombers, including four-engine types, dropped aerial bombs aimlessly. The once-renowned Stuka even tried shallow dive bombing against them. Fortunately, the 305th returned to base without loss.

Bad weather plagued the group during its industrial attacks the early part of December although it was a busy month for the weary crews.

On the day before Christmas, the first of the "V" weapons' sites, referred to as "military installations in France," were attacked.

The year ended with a mission to Ludwigshafen on the thirtieth—a routine pathfinder attack—and a New Year's Eve trip to Cognac.

The 422nd Bombardment Squadron did valiant work in a specific type of operation which had started on the eighth of September. Before beginning independent operations, they joined the R.A.F. on a night mission to

Distinguished Unit Citation

establish whether the Fortress was qualified for this type of operation.

They flew eight missions, after the B-17's had been properly adapted for night flights, dropping bombs on selected targets. It was soon apparent that the B-17 was ill-fitted for night bombing operations but ideally designed for psychological warfare. After the initial test runs, leaflets were carried instead of explosives.

The squadron made its first leaflet raid October 7 and thereafter continued them whenever weather permitted.

Ordinarily, between five and ten B-17's were sent out, each going to selected areas, flying alone and unescorted.

The leaflets were dropped over cities and towns in occupied Europe, sometimes giving instructions to the French people, at other times bringing the latest, unslanted war news to the Dutch.

The 422nd Squadron carried on this invaluable work until June 1944, when it returned to regular daytime missions.

Colonel Ernest H. Lawson, taking command of the group after Colonel Wilson was transferred, called in the staff after receiving a letter from division headquarters.

"I have a personal commendation from General Anderson," he said. "I want it posted in every area because all members of the group helped to earn it.

"He says, in part, the 305th has compiled a brilliant combat record, including such successful and outstanding missions as the attacks on Vegesack, Gdynia, Knaben, and Schweinfurt." He paused. "Let me add my own personal congratulations."

Lawson leaned back in his chair reflectively. "Nineteen

forty-four will see an intensification of the bombing of Germany. There isn't much time, but we've got to establish an intensive training program for the many replacement crews now reporting in."

Lieutenant Colonel William E. Sault, group operations officer, nodded his head soberly. "It will take time to train new crews to maintain our combat effectiveness."

Sault studied the teletype message he had just received from headquarters, 40th Combat Wing, at 7:55 P.M. on January 10.

He noted with surprise that it called for a maximum effort the following day. All aircraft were to be loaded with 12 five-hundred-pound general purpose bombs.

"Sergeant," he called. "Alert the squadrons for a 5:10 A.M. briefing."

He glanced anxiously at the operations board listing aircraft in commission. "We should be able to get two formations off," he said to himself.

After studying the field order, he realized it was to be the first deep penetration of the Reich under visual bombing conditions since October 14. He whistled shrilly to himself, remembering Schweinfurt.

Three divisions would take part in the massive attack, including twelve combat wings of B-17's and B-24's, and the 1st Bombardment Division would lead the entire Eighth Air Force into Central Germany to attack vital aircraft factories. Their target was Halberstadt.

Major Shaffer was grim-faced as he waited for take-off. A B-17 had blown a tire so the formation was held on the ground an additional seven minutes until the aircraft was pulled aside.

Distinguished Unit Citation

In command of the lead group formation, he took off at 8:17 A.M. and waited while the formation formed over Podington. Only fifteen B-17's joined him, and he exchanged a worried look with his copilot, Lieutenant B.M. Davey.

They had a pathfinder crew along, but they hoped to bomb visually. These specially equipped pathfinder B-17's could bomb without seeing the target by computing dropping angles from simultaneous transmission of radar beams from two stations in England.

Davey was tight-lipped as he turned to Shaffer. "I understand the Germans have enlarged their force of fighters in Holland and Northwest Germany."

"It could be rough," the major said. "There are at least one hundred and twenty day fighters available plus all the night outfits."

They droned across the Channel on time, making all control points.

"I'm going to stay at thirteen thousand feet," Shaffer said, "to keep out of that soup." He pointed to the thick clouds above them.

Near the coast, however, he climbed steadily to bombing altitude of seventeen thousand feet and proceeded towards the target.

In the vicinity of Dummer Lake, the fighters appeared and rockets flamed at them.

Weather conditions were so bad that Shaffer called for the pathfinder crew to take over. Just as the switch was being made, the bombardier called excitedly, "There's a break in the clouds! I can see factory buildings."

"Make a visual run," Shaffer ordered.

Flak filled the sky around them, bursting with red flashes so close to the B-17's they all instinctively flinched.

German fighters ignored their own flak and slashed viciously through the formations.

Shaffer took a quick check at his formation. No one had gone down! The rest of the division, he saw with mounting concern, was receiving brutal damage, and crumpled B-17's were going down in numbers he hadn't seen since Schweinfurt.

Many of the sturdy Forts were so mangled that he looked at them with awe. How they kept flying was more than he could imagine.

Major R.E. Smith, heading the 40th Wing's low group, had eighteen B-17's over the target, but his bombardier couldn't find anything on which to make a run because of the bad weather, so they had a three hundred and sixty degree turn.

Lieutenant Lockwood, in the nose, spotted a hole. "Bombardier to pilot. I can see a marshalling yard below me. I'm going to bomb it."

"Roger," the pilot said.

Fighter attacks slammed through the formation while the run was made. Smith sat in the pilot's seat literally appalled by the severity of the enemy attacks as B-17's exploded in mid-air, descending as huge balls of fire with portions of wings and tails flying in all directions.

The gunners fought back doggedly until the fighters at last were driven away and the Germans headed for another formation which they hoped would not be such a tough adversary.

On the return trip, the enemy fighters continued to concentrate their efforts on the 1st Division, and, with forty-two bombers down, the ragged formations fought back with a heroism that inflicted heavy losses on the enemy.

Both Lawson and Sault were puffy-eyed and exhausted when they sat down that night to discuss the mission.

"We were lucky," Sault said. "We didn't lose a crew, but all divisions lost sixty bombers. What happened to the fighter support?"

"Bad weather hampered their operations," Lawson said. "They're not to blame."

"The Germans took advantage of the relative vulnerability of the lead division," Sault said, "and concentrated their most powerful forces against us. The scale of the enemy attack is graphically shown by the four hundred enemy encounters recorded by the division."

"The gunners did a magnificent job," Lawson said proudly. "They met these continuous attacks with accurate fire. I understand the division claims two hundred and ten enemy aircraft shot down. Without a doubt, that's the largest number ever claimed by any division of the Eighth Air Force on any one mission. On top of that, forty-three probably were destroyed and eighty-four damaged."

There was no question in anyone's mind at headquarters that the success of the strike, under exceptionally difficult conditions, was due solely to the tenacious fighting spirit of these young Americans.

German fighter pilots, who had their own wounds to lick, were the first to agree.

When General Anderson saw the strike photographs, he was tremendously uplifted. Although the weather was a limiting factor, the complete results were most satisfactory.

The terrible toll of bombers was shocking, but he knew their sacrifices would help shorten the war by reducing German aircraft production.

At Oschersleben, site of the most important remaining plant of the Focke-Wulfe complex, strike photographs showed a compact pattern of bombs covering the target area. The main machine shop was set on fire at the end of the attack as a result of several direct hits. All plant units, Anderson noted, received hits, and the damage was most severe in the main plant area.

The largest concentration of bombs fell just east of the plant area at the Junkers wing manufacturing plant at Halberstadt during the first bomber attacks. The second wave, however, scored a heavy concentration on a large workshop and office building. Two of the five large workshops actually received severe damage.

The 1st Bombardment Division, including the 305th, received a well-earned Distinguished Unit Citation for the raid.

Five B-17's of the 422nd Squadron dropped four million, eight hundred thousand leaflets over France from twenty to twenty-four thousand five hundred feet the night of January 10/11 with perfect immunity. In significant contrast to the day mission, the night intruders met no opposition from either fighters or flak.

CHAPTER 10

A Nightmarish Encounter with Death

A SOFT-SPOKEN YOUNG lieutenant from Alabama, who had received his wings less than a year ago, sat with his crew during the briefing on February 20.

William R. Lawley, Jr., had entered the Army as a private but he had always wanted to fly, and finally the coveted chance had come. He had never regretted the rigorous training, and now he had his own crew with one of the most famous groups in England.

While the briefing officers droned on, describing the myriad details of the mission to Leipzig, he whispered to his bombardier, Lieutenant Harry G. Mason, "Doesn't sound too bad, Harry."

"Who knows?" Mason said with a shrug. "You never can tell about a strike into Germany."

They were both to remember these casual words later on.

Three divisions, the first, second, and third were scheduled to carry out the largest force of heavy bombers and fighters ever employed on a daylight bombing operation.

They would strike at the heart of Germany's aircraft production plants. The field order called for thirteen combat wings of Fortresses and three of Liberators to attack ME-109, ME-110, JU-88, and JU-188 assembly plants.

Supported by seventeen groups of USAAF fighters and sixteen squadrons of R.A.F. Spitfires and Mustangs, it was a daring mission that foretold the massive strikes yet to come.

The 1st Bombardment Division, including the 305th, was assigned the three plants of the Erla Complex, manufacturing ME-109's in the Leipzig area.

"Hope we can knock it out," Lawley said. "There'll be less fighters to shoot at later on."

"I wish I could lead it," Mason said wistfully.

Although visual bombing was anticipated, a pathfinder aircraft was assigned to each formation to aid in navigation.

Aircraft of the 305th formed the lead group of the 40th Combat Wing's B-formation over Podington where assembly was accomplished at nine thousand feet.

They moved out on course, and the low and high groups moved into position.

"Hope we don't have these thick clouds over the target," Lawley said to his copilot anxiously.

"If we do, we'll have to come back again."

They broke into the clear fifteen minutes from the target and, with excitement mounting, they slowly started down those last anxious miles to the target itself.

A Nightmarish Encounter with Death

There was only light and inaccurate flak at first, but, as they neared the bomb release line, it became more intense although it remained wide of its target.

"Tail gunner to crew. Fighters at 6 o'clock!"

Lawley's facial muscles twitched. There was a long minute of silence with no further word.

"Pilot to tail gunner. What's going on?" he said anxiously.

"These boys are just playing," the tail gunner said with a chuckle. "They don't mean business."

"Watch them," Lawley warned. "They'll be back."

Mason hit the release lever when he saw the leader's five hundred pounders part from the aircraft up ahead. He peered anxiously at the ground.

"Hey, skipper," he called to Lawley, "the target is covered completely with bombs." And then, with anxious concern, "I wonder what happened. Our bombs didn't drop."

Lawley had time only for a quick acknowledgment because twenty fighters appeared as if out of nowhere and the B-17 shuddered with the impact of their guns.

Lawley desperately tried to hold his crippled Fort in formation, but it was no use. He started to say something to his copilot, but, to his horror, he found that he had been killed by the shattering 20 mm. cannon blast that had smashed into the cockpit.

Mason called with quick urgency. "We've got an engine on fire!"

Lawley was much too busy to acknowledge because it was evident that most of his controls had been shot away, and, with all the skill he had ever acquired as a pilot, he manfully struggled to regain mastery of his fifty-five-thousand-pound bomber.

It was then he realized he had been wounded. In the excitement of the moment he had felt sharp pains, but only when he wiped his hand across his face and saw the blood was he fully aware that he had been hit by the exploding shell.

The airplane would not respond to his mightiest efforts to pull it out of its dive. Blood covered the instruments and windshield, and it was impossible to see out of the airplane.

Suddenly, he realized that the dead copilot's body, slumped over the wheel, was interfering with the controls. He unstrapped his seat belt, hurried to the right side, and frantically removed the body.

Sickened by the ghastly sight on the flight deck and ignoring his own painful wounds, he flung himself back into the pilot's seat and, with every muscle in his body straining at the utmost, he gradually pulled the airplane out of its dive.

"You've got to get rid of those bombs," Lawley yelled to Mason.

"They won't release!" Mason said frantically. "The racks must be frozen."

With a full bomb load, the plane was difficult to maneuver. Lawley decided their only chance was to bail out.

He called each station but was appalled by what he heard. Eight members of the crew were wounded.

Sergeant Thomas A. Dempsey, the radio operator, said, "We can't bail out! Two gunners are so seriously wounded they can't leave the ship."

Lawley made a decision. Come what may he would ride this tortured airplane as far as it would go. His

A Nightmarish Encounter with Death 117

decision was clear and irrevocable. No pilot ever abandoned his crewmates.

He anxiously watched the flaming engine. He tried the extinguisher, and, to his relief, the flames died down.

Now that he had elected to remain with the plane and bring them back safely if it was humanly possible, his emotions calmed down.

His first thought was for the crew. "Pilot to crew. All those who are physically able, bail out! That's an order!"

No one elected to leave the stricken B-17, and he smiled proudly at their grim determination to stay with him despite the ultimate cost.

Another engine caught fire as enemy fighters swarmed at them, while the gunners fought back doggedly with a savagery they didn't think was in them.

Again, flying with his left hand, he pressed the extinguisher and, with a sob of relief, saw the fire die down.

The fighters finally abandoned the gallant bomber that refused to call it quits.

Mason looked anxiously at the pilot after he had crawled to the flight deck. He was covered with blood from the streaming wounds on his face, and it was all Mason could do to look at him.

"I finally salvoed the bombs," Mason said. Lawley looked ghastly to him. He expected any moment to see the pilot slump over the controls. Lawley, noticing his expression, said weakly, "I'm all right."

Mason grew more concerned because he could see that Lawley was near a state of complete collapse due to the loss of blood, the shock of what had happened to them, and the energy he had expended in keeping control of the plane.

Lawley refused to leave his seat behind the wheel, however, until he collapsed from sheer exhaustion.

Mason grabbed the controls and headed the plane for England. He had washed out of flying school so he was appalled by the prospect of getting them to a safe landing.

When they appeared over the coast and Mason spotted a small fighter base, he shook Lawley into consciousness. Only he could land the bomber, and it was imperative that Lawley be revived for the last desperate minutes until they were again safely on the ground.

Lawley, mustering every bit of superhuman energy of which he was capable, grabbed the wheel and took control of the Fortress.

An engine coughed, and the prop started to windmill. "That engine's out of gas," Lawley said thickly. "Feather it."

Just then, another engine caught fire as they were on the final approach.

Lawley pointed the nose frantically towards the end of the runway, and the Flying Fortress careened in for a crash landing.

Fire trucks and ambulances immediately were on the scene to put out the fire and remove the seriously wounded.

For Lawley, and his nightmarish encounter with death in the skies, the United States paid its greatest tribute. He was awarded the Medal of Honor for conspicuous gallantry and intrepidity in action above and beyond the call of duty.

For their individual heroism, both Sergeant Dempsey and Lieutenant Mason received Silver Stars.

The 305th had attacked the target with thirty-six aircraft, and two of them were lost to enemy action.

A Nightmarish Encounter with Death 119

It was the most successful mission to date by the Eighth Air Force. Considering the depth of the penetration into the Reich, an outstanding feature of this operation was its small loss, numbering twenty-one bombers and four fighters. This was due in large measure to the excellence of the fighter escort, but it also was apparent the German Air Force had been surprised by the employment of such a large force, particularly after the large-scale R.A.F. attack on Leipzig the previous night.

At Leipzig, two hundred and thirty-nine B-17's had saturated the three factory targets. Each of the aircraft factories bordering Mockau Airfield received extensive damage. The Erla Maschinenwerk fighter assembly factory, the most important of these objectives, received direct hits on its principal assembly shop, and the second large assembly shop was left on fire. Flight hangars were included among the other buildings sustaining hits.

The Allgemeine Transport bomber assembly plant received a heavy concentration of hits, and subsequent reconnaissance photographs showed two of the three main assembly shops burning and the other partly burned out.

The Junkers assembly and repair plant sustained extensive damage from direct hits and fire. At the German Air Force station, hits were obtained on one of the large buildings.

In addition to the damage to plants and buildings, numerous aircraft in various parts of the field were affected.

Available evidence indicates there were approximately two hundred and seventy-five sorties flown against the operation. Approximately two-thirds of the enemy aircraft were single-engine fighters, and the remainder twin engine.

The scale of the enemy effort was not commensurate with the size of the bomber forces. Weather conditions over Holland and the possible exhaustion of night fighters by the heavy R.A.F. attack on Leipzig may offer partial explanation.

In addition, R.A.F. wireless intelligence services indicated the bombers which crossed over Denmark were suspected of being the main effort, possibly directed against Berlin. As a result, the German controller dispatched a substantial portion of his strength to meet this threat.

This mission was the first of a series in the so-called "Big Week" of February 20-25 which saw repeated attacks against the German air-frame industry.

Eighth Air Force commanders gave fighter planes a number one priority to endeavor to destroy at the source the potential danger to future bomber formations. Upon its results, they knew, might hinge the ultimate success of deep penetrations into the Reich.

One sure method of keeping the fighters off the backs of the American bombers, LeMay reminded commanders, was to destroy them before they were delivered to operational units. In this respect, February 1944 was a memorable month for the thousands who were yet to match their guns with the Germans before the war ended.

CHAPTER 11

Berlin!

DURING THE MONTH of March, the Army Air Forces dropped the greatest weight of bombs ever dropped in a single month on Germany. The average was over one thousand tons a day by the combined groups of planes sent out to attack the continent. They represented units of the Eighth and Ninth Air Forces flying from England, and the Fifteenth Air Force from Italy.

The 1st Air Division had attacked the Alfted Teves Aircraft component factory in Frankfurt on the second of March with only fair results.

On the following day, the primary target was the Erkner Ball Bearing plant near Berlin. The 305th joined the 40th Combat Wing, but bad weather forced abandonment of the mission.

In a determined effort to bomb Berlin, the target for the fourth of March again was the suburb of Erkner.

The Incredible 305th

Assembly was carried out under difficult circumstances due to weather, and the final division assembly was never accomplished. Some units of the 40th were unable to keep visual contact with the rest of the division so they reluctantly abandoned the mission at the enemy coast.

The other units proceeded into Germany, but cloud conditions became worse and all but one wing decided to abandon the mission. A one hundred and eighty degree turn was executed by the other wings to pick targets of opportunity.

Colonel C.R. Storrie, command pilot of the lead group of the 40th Combat Wing, relaxed briefly after take-off on the sixth of March for another try at a large-scale daylight attack against Berlin.

It had been a sober briefing with all individuals aware of the tremendous significance of the event and no one inclined to discount the opposition they would face. They were certain Goering's boys would dispute their passage every foot of the way.

Eleven combat wings of B-17's and three of 24's had taken off. They would have effective escort to enable them to fight their way to the German capital because nineteen groups of fighters had been assigned for their protection.

Storrie knew Berlin air defenses had been expecting this attack since the first two-day raids had been failures.

Little opposition was encountered until they were forty-five minutes from Berlin.

Lieutenant Drake in the left-hand pilot's seat saw them first: "110's, twelve o'clock, level!"

Twenty-five of them made frontal sweeps at the formation, and holes began to appear in wings and fuselages.

Storrie quickly cast his eyes at the formation. They were holding together tightly, and no one seemed in difficulty.

He watched the Nazi fighters with admiration. They braved the massed fire of the composite group's guns and hurtled through the formation. Then, turning behind them, they swept around in front again for more attacks.

"You've got to hand it to them," Drake said grimly. "They sure can fly."

The attacks persisted until the IP was reached, and now Storrie had a decision to make because it appeared the ball-bearing plant was obscured by clouds.

"Storrie to bombardier. Can you bomb the primary?"

"No, sir, I've tried my best to spot the aiming point through a hole in the clouds," Lieutenant Haas said.

"We've come a long way," Storrie said grimly. "Drop them on Berlin!"

During the run, the fighters were so numerous and the Fortresses under such constant attack that Storrie lost count of actions.

Over the target area, he figured there must be one hundred ME-110's, FW-190's, and ME-109's, each of which seemed to make at least one pass at them. They came level, wave after wave, and it seemed impossible one of their Fortresses hadn't been knocked down. They clung together for protection and fought back with unbelievable intensity.

"The 88's are firing rockets again," Drake said in a shaky voice.

The dive bombers stood off at one thousand yards on their left and fired salvos which miraculously failed to find a target.

Just before bombs away, the attacks mounted in ferocity as the German fighters lashed particularly at the lead ship. They came so close to the Fortresses in their swing across that they seemed to skim over the top turrets.

"Our fighter escort is badly outnumbered," Storrie said grimly. "There are just too many of the enemy."

Bombardier Haas quickly spotted his bombs in the northeast center of Berlin and went back to his guns.

Although the flak was heavy, the German fighters ignored it and continued to follow the departing groups as they pulled away from the burning city.

Looking back, Storrie saw a Fortress blow up over the target as one of the anti-aircraft guns found its mark.

The low group, Storrie saw, was following them closely after making its bombing run. Another composite group, led by Lieutenant Goodin, held formation closely despite persistent attacks.

On withdrawal, Storrie watched the following formations proceed to the target. His throat was dry and his hands shook as he saw two B-17's disintegrate. He watched closely for parachutes, but there were none.

Another B-17 peeled off from a formation at eighteen thousand feet and drifted helplessly through the clouds while four men parachuted out.

Storrie pointed to one particular formation. "They're catching it worse than the others."

A wing section blew off the first B-17, and the aircraft flamed brightly as four men jumped to safety. A second B-17 pulled out of formation with an engine on fire and then, with an awesome explosion, blew itself to pieces. Still a third Fortress rocketed out of the formation and headed for the huge city, but this time all but one man managed to jump.

The sky was full of blazing bombers as they swung in a wide sweep of the city.

Drake watched the deadly battle in shocked silence. He saw two B-17's go down and spotted only two parachutes. A Fort went into a vertical dive from sixteen thousand feet and exploded fifteen miles away. No one had a chance to get out.

"I've never seen such savage attacks," Drake said. "How can we get out of this alive?"

"We'll fight our way out!" Storrie said. "We're fortunate. They haven't hurt us yet."

Although other wings suffered grievous losses, the 305th did not lose a single airplane. In a magnificent display of raw courage and skill, they had challenged the Luftwaffe over their capital and come away unscathed.

Among the three bombardment divisions participating in the Berlin mission, four hundred and thirteen B-17's had dropped nine hundred and seventy tons of bombs. The B-14's released five hundred and thirty additional tons on the Greater Berlin area.

Although the bombing was scattered, there were good concentrations in the southeastern suburbs of the city, especially in the Zehlendorf area. Bombs also fell in the Spandau section where the main railway was severed.

The 1st Division, which led the attack, and particularly the first two combat wings, received the worst enemy opposition.

The 3rd Division, which came after them, also received the full viciousness of what the German fighters had to offer. Their two combat wings in the middle suffered the most.

By the time the 2nd Division had arrived, the German

fighters were either exhausted or down to refuel because they met very weak enemy opposition.

The Eighth suffered grievous losses with fifty-three B-17's and sixteen B-24's lost on the mission, most of them due to fighter attacks.

Claims of enemy aircraft destroyed by the gunners attested to the ferocity of the combat. The 1st and 3rd Divisions claimed eighty-eight destroyed, forty-four probably destroyed, and sixty-six damaged. The 2nd Division, because they had been fortunate in meeting only slight opposition put in claims for five destroyed.

It was unfortunate that weather conditions were such as to prevent bombing of the three high-priority targets in Berlin. The plan was an excellent one if the elements had been helpful.

The decision had been made for the 1st Division to attack the Erkner Ball Bearing plant with five combat wings. An aerial engine factory had been chosen for the 2nd Division, and the 3rd Division was to have struck the electrical equipment factory which made magneto needles and accessories for airplanes.

During the week, Sergeant Lee C. Gordon returned to England after finally making his escape from German prison camps.

After imprisonment following his bail-out over Wilhemshaven in February 1943, he related how he made his first attempt at freedom in the company of another American with whom he leaped from a moving train while being transferred to another camp. Capture quickly followed this poorly planned escape.

For the next attempt, Gordon said he had made a

careful study of all possible means of escape, of dangers, and routes out of Germany.

"I decided the route to Switzerland was most promising," he said, "so I dressed as a Bavarian boy and started on my journey."

This carefully planned scientific manner of escape was wasted by a very simple mistake.

"I was tired after a long day's cycling," he said, "so I decided to leave the road before sundown. I bedded down in a haystack, but a guard who had been watching the road saw me pull off and climb the haystack. He became suspicious and, upon investigation, promptly captured me."

If Gordon had waited until dark before quitting the road, it is possible he would have passed unnoticed.

He described his last escape attempt in the company of a British captain and how, with the aid of the French, he succeeded in reaching the United Kingdom.

Following the last Berlin mission, replacements in both men and equipment came to the group. The whole division received fourteen new crews, but they failed to make up for losses so the total crew strength declined.

Colonel Lawson, after receiving a division study of missions which failed because of weather conditions, discussed it with his staff. "The report covers only sixteen outstanding cases of the past year, but the conclusion is obvious," he said. "On all missions where bad weather was a factor, bombing results were insignificant compared to the trouble of sending the bombers out and, in some cases, compared to the losses on the attempted mission."

He turned sympathetically to the group weather officer. "You have done an outstanding job," he said. "Perhaps even more careful observations of over-all weather conditions will assist us in paying larger dividends in men, material, and time saved."

This was easier said than done because the long-suffering weather officers had an impossible task, but they promised to do whatever was humanly possible.

With the opening of the second week of March, the attack on Germany continued with a most successful mission to Berlin March 8. The primary target at Erkner again was the ball-bearing works.

Sixteen miles southeast of the center of Berlin, the plant was capable of producing thirty thousand ball bearings a day. Estimates listed it as providing 7 per cent of the total enemy production.

After an eminently successful mission, Lawson told the crews, "It was the smoothest mission you have flown, probably the nearest to being flown as briefed as any of you have made."

For the mission, a total of two hundred and forty-seven aircraft had been scheduled to fly in the 1st Division. Only one failed to take off, twenty-two returned early, and four were lost to enemy action.

Swedish newspapers, which published eyewitness accounts of the attack, remarked that Berliners were astonished at the accuracy of the bombing. Although the plant was not totally destroyed, extremely great damage was done.

The Berlin area was attacked the following day. The Heinkel plant at Oranienburg was set for the strike, but

Berlin!

complete cloud cover made it necessary to drop the bombs on the city of Berlin.

During the third week of March, a very heavy program of bombing started until four important missions were completed by the 305th. They attacked three targets in Germany and one in Northern France. These were airfield installations but of vital concern to the planners for the coming invasion of Normandy. From now on, they would concern themselves primarily with destroying the German Air Force and its installations on the ground.

The month closed on a highly important statistical note. The striking power of the American Air Forces, for the first time in the history of the war, dropped a tonnage of bombs that was about the same as that dropped by the R.A.F.

It was an amount greater than the total tonnage dropped by this Air Force in the first year of its operational activity.

The combined attacks of the Allied air fleets were in themselves the opening of the long-expected second front in the west.

The extent of the bombing was not achieved by expending in a gigantic effort all the resources of the Air Force for a single desperate month of bombing. It never taxed its strength, and in the succeeding months further growth was expected in the destructive power of both the British and American Air Forces.

So large and formidable had this combined force become that the Germans faced a painful dilemma. If they sent their total force of interceptors to meet the formations, the fighter support and the terrific fire of the bombers would practically annihilate the German fighter force.

If they did not send interceptors to meet the formations, the bombers would be free to attack any target they chose with only slight losses. This also would cut down the ability of Germany to produce fighters.

Lawson told the staff, "The Germans are forced into a position where only occasionally can their fighters be sent up to intercept our bombers. In almost every case, this probably will be when our escort fighters are absent temporarily.

"German fighter pilots have a dim future," he said, "and it will get worse. Any question of superiority in the air was answered the day we flew to the very heart of Germany and destroyed one of their most important plants, the ball-bearing works at Erkner, and were not attacked by the full might of Germany's fighter strength."

He paused thoughtfully. "Now that the German Air Force cannot or will not defend its own capital, it has gone a longer way down the inevitable road to complete destruction."

CHAPTER 12

The Nation's Highest Award

THE BRIEFING ROOM quieted down as Colonel Lawson rose to add a few comments before the crews boarded their B-17's on April 11.

"Today we are part of a large-scale effort to wipe out six FW-190 and Junker assembly plants deep in Central and Eastern Europe."

They sat silently, sobered by the thought of the opposition they might meet.

"Almost a thousand heavy bombers have been assigned to the job," Lawson said. "The routes to the targets constitute a double thrust into enemy territory, and both the penetration and withdrawal courses have been planned carefully to disrupt the enemy defenses.

"We can make a significant contribution, battle-hardened as we are after countless strikes into Germany. Good luck to you all."

The Incredible 305th
• • •

Lieutenant Edward S. Michael gathered his crew around him, and they walked quietly to the flight line.

For him, assignment to the 305th was a dream come true. He had wanted to fly ever since he was ten years old and saw his first big air show at the Curtis Wright airfield in his home town of Chicago.

His biggest thrill in those early years was when he had impulsively asked Colonel Roscoe Turner for his autograph. In those days, Turner was the hottest pilot after setting a new world record of two hundred and fifty-three miles an hour.

After shaking hands with people like Jimmy Doolittle and the three pilots of an Air Corps flying team renowned for their act of tying three biplanes together with ten-foot lengths of rope and accomplishing acrobatics, he would walk home with his heart in the clouds.

Through the years, he had idolized every one of these pilots. As long as he could remember, he felt that every pilot who crashed and died wanted to go that way because, he reasoned, when one loves to fly there couldn't be a better way.

In 1934, as a sophomore in high school, he had dreamed of college, but the depression made this impossible. He decided to get a job and help his family.

Through a friend, he was hired as a drill-press operator and worked as a caddy at the golf course on Sundays.

His dreams of flying remained vivid, but there seemed no possible way to raise the money for lessons.

But, by careful husbanding of his resources, he started private lessons in July of 1940 at a small flying strip four miles from home.

The Nation's Highest Award 133

He managed to solo before he enlisted in the Army Air Corps in November of 1940. Due to his inadequate finances, he had accumulated only twenty hours of flying time, but they were some of the happiest hours of his life.

In the Air Corps, he served initially as an airplane mechanic at Wheeler Field, Hawaii, while he studied for his aviation cadet entrance examinations. When he felt prepared, he took a test that was equivalent to two years of college.

December 5, 1941, he found a note on the squadron bulletin board advising all those who had taken the test to report to the First Sergeant on Sunday morning.

That was the day the Japanese attacked, so it was months before he learned that he had failed the cadet examination. He studied all the harder because now he had a stronger purpose in life, remembering his friends who had died at Wheeler.

His intensive efforts were rewarded finally, and he returned to the mainland as a cadet in July of 1942.

Graduating with the April, 1943, class he decided he wanted to become a bomber pilot.

"What are you smiling about, Eddie?" his copilot, Lieutenant Westberg, said.

"Just remembering," Michael said. "And reminding myself what a lucky guy I am to head such a crew. Board up!"

One by one, the Flying Fortresses took off until twenty-six airplanes were headed towards Germany in two box formations.

"I doubt if we're going to have any luck today," Michael said later. He swept his arm in a wide circle. "This cloud cover appears to lie over our primary and secondary targets."

He called Lieutenant Leiber in the bombardier's compartment. "Search for a target of opportunity. Any military installation will do."

They were east of Berlin by now. Westberg saw them first. "Fighters!" he yelled. "There must be a hundred of them," he said breathlessly as they flashed by them.

Michael felt the shock of bullets tearing through thin aluminum. "They're singling us out," he said tensely. "We're in for it!"

The enemy fighters ignored their own intense flak and the Allied fighter escort as they tore at the formation with blazing cannons.

Michael felt the B-17 shudder beneath him during one savage assault. After calling all stations, he learned the aircraft was riddled from nose to tail.

The plane momentarily went out of control, and, despite his efforts to hold it in the protective custody of the formation, it descended in a sickening plunge while a large number of Nazi fighters followed it down.

A cannon shell exploded in the cockpit. Almost blinded by the shock of the blast which wrecked his instruments and blew out the side window, he found time to cast an anxious glance at Westberg.

His copilot grimaced with pain from streaming wounds, but he signaled that he would carry on.

Michael then felt the pain in his right thigh. When he explored with his fingers, they were sticky with blood when he held them up in front of him.

Hydraulic lines had been slashed, and the fluid filmed

the windshield so visibility was impossible.

With smoke filling the cockpit, he fought the controls doggedly but they at first failed to respond.

The altimeter was gone, but he knew that he must be close to the ground so he renewed his efforts to bring the Fortress out of its steep dive. Just when he had given up hope, the controls responded.

"There's a fire in the bomb bay!" the radio operator said hysterically. "Cannon shells also have ignited some of the incendiaries."

With a full load of bombs and considerable gas left in the tanks, the danger of fire enveloping the plane and the tanks exploding seemed imminent.

He called Leiber hurriedly. "Try the emergency lever! Get those bombs out or we've had it!"

The bombardier frantically tried to salvo, but it was no use.

Michael yelled, "Bail out! Bail out! We're on fire!"

Seven of the crew quickly exited the bomber, but seeing the bombardier still firing his guns, he called urgently, "Get out, Leiber!"

The bombardier looked for his parachute and was appalled to find it was riddled with 20 mm. fragments.

He hauled the useless parachute to the cockpit and, without saying a word, showed it to Michael.

The pilot had no intention of abandoning his bombardier to certain death. He decided their only hope was a crash landing.

Completely disregarding his own painful and profusely bleeding wounds, but thinking only of the safety of the remaining crew members, he evaded the enemy by using violent evasive action despite the battered condition of the airplane.

Much to their relief, Leiber finally salvoed the smoldering bombs.

After they had been under sustained fighter attack for forty-five minutes, Michael lost the persistent fighters in a cloud bank.

Upon emerging, an accurate barrage of flak caused him to come down to treetop level where flak towers poured a continuous rain of fire at the plane.

He continued into France, realizing that at any moment a crash landing might be necessary, but trying to get as far as possible to increase the escape possibilities if a safe landing could be achieved.

Westberg watched Michael with a creeping sensation of horror as the pilot's blood formed in pools on the floor of the cockpit.

When Michael lost consciousness, Westberg grabbed the wheel and held the riddled bomber on an uneven course for England.

He spotted an R.A.F. field near the coast and headed for it. Some semblance of life returned to Lieutenant Michael who insisted upon taking command of his airplane. "I can handle it," he said with an effort. "Report on the airplane's condition."

"The gear is useless," Westberg said. "The fire in the bomb bay is out, but both doors are jammed open."

"If I only had flight instruments," Michael said desperately. "Both the altimeter and the airspeed indicator are out."

"I forgot to tell you," Westberg said, "the flaps won't come down."

On the approach, they only had a chance for a desperate glance at each other. Despite apparently insurmountable obstacles, Michael belly-landed the airplane successfully.

It was a day they would long remember, but an even greater day came for Lieutenant Michael when the President of the United States hung the Medal of Honor around his neck.

For their heroic assistance in bringing the airplane back to England, Lieutenant Westberg and Lieutenant Leiber received the nation's third highest award—the Silver Star.

Lawson read the mission analysis to the staff. "There were six hundred and forty-three B-17's and two hundred B-24's over Germany." He looked up and his eyes reflected his deepest emotions. "Quite a contrast to operations a year ago," he said.

"The enemy contrived one of his most severe and well-co-ordinated defenses that was marked by the skillful handling of a considerable number of day fighters in the Stettin area, and in the Hanover-Oschersleben area," he said. "Final reports indicate a total of fifty-two B-17's and twelve B-24's were lost."

A total of twenty-one fighter groups supported the day's operations, including four Ninth Air Force groups. Generally good support was accorded the bomber formations, and, on the whole, escort was carried out according to plan.

The brunt of the enemy air opposition was borne by the fighter groups supporting the Sorau-Cottbus force. Of total fighter claims against air-borne enemy aircraft of fifty-one destroyed, these groups accounted for forty-eight destroyed.

It was estimated that approximately two hundred enemy aircraft participated in interception efforts, of which approximately sixty were twin-engine fighters. In addition, forty of the single-engine aircraft were believed to have made double sorties.

The bomber forces achieved good to excellent results at most of the struck plants so their losses were not in vain.

CHAPTER 13

D-Day

A SPECIAL ITEM haunted the minds of everyone in the group throughout the month of April. In every place where people gathered there was wild speculation on the date when the ground forces would invade the continent.

If the speculation on the invasion of Europe by land was a matter of conjecture, there was no doubt as to the opening of the second front in the air war. That front was wide open!

After eight days of spring rain and fog, the sun appeared and stayed out for the rest of the month.

All day long, all night long, formations of planes could be seen or heard daily overhead. Along the southeast coast of England, people watched the endless procession moving out by the thousands to strike at the industrial and communications centers of Germany and the occupied countries.

Bombers and fighters struck at the railroads and airfields of France and the manufacturing centers of Germany. From Italy, too, the bombers flew deeply into enemy territory. While the Eighth and Ninth Air Forces struck from the west, softening up the Westwall, the Fifteenth Air Force was cutting at the rail junctions in Germany from the east.

From Rumania to Poland to the Pas de Calais, British and American bombs were falling on Fortress Europe, cutting deeply into Germany's reserves while the stature of the Allied Air Forces grew daily.

The aerial assault against the aircraft industry in Germany was taken up again on the eighteenth of April when the 305th took part in an attack on the FW-190 plants.

The accurate flak barrage showed that the forbidding reputation of Kassel's ground defenses was still potent, but eighteen bombers placed their bombs on the plant. In spite of the flak, all aircraft returned.

Increasing concern for the German guided missile and rocket installations attracted the attention of the planners when two sub-groups of twelve B-17's were sent to France and dropped a concentration on an important target area.

The 305th's next foray was directed at the Hamm Marshalling Yards where a considerable portion of Germany's eastern rail traffic was handled. The entire yard was blanketed with bursts.

The next target failed miserably to live up to the comic implications of its name—Oberpfaffenhofen. The flak was intense, and matters were further complicated by one hundred and fifty enemy aircraft who were in a highly aggressive mood.

On this raid, the group was leading the combat wing and a notable performance was turned in by Lieutenant

Wynne, lead bombardier, who was wounded in the eye just before reaching the bomb-release line. In spite of this, he managed to crawl back to his sight and get his bombs in the target area.

Apparently feeling that no month was complete without at least one trip to Berlin, the group bombed the German capital on the twenty-ninth, using pathfinder methods to penetrate the undercast. No industrial installations were hit, but considerable satisfaction was derived from the extensive damage inflicted on the Reich's Air Ministry buildings.

The Fortresses of the 422nd Squadron, which flew at night dropping leaflets in the occupied countries of Europe, were out sixteen times during April. Their targets ranged from Trondheim in Norway to Lyon and Toulouse in France.

The total of cities included eighty-seven, mostly in France. Holland and Belgium received their share of newspapers and pamphlets, which were prepared by specialists in the art of psychological warfare. It was a satisfaction to the crews to know that these publications, telling the straight news stories of the war, were eagerly awaited in occupied Europe.

April was the greatest month for bombing to that date with an estimated eighty thousand tons dropped by the combined USAAF and R.A.F. forces on targets all over Europe. It was the first month since war began that the United States Air Forces came out definitely on top in the laudable rivalry with the R.A.F. as to which could drop the most bombs on the targets of occupied Europe.

No matter who won the match each month, Hitler lost. It was significant, of course, that the month surpassed all other months of the war for tonnage of bombs, but what was more significant was the knowledge that even now the maximum striking power of the Allied Air Forces was yet to be attained.

Germany's plans to attain its maximum peak of power in the spring of 1944 were not only frustrated, but a completely opposite condition developed. The centers of production had been hit heavily, the front-line strength of the Luftwaffe was cut to a dangerously low level, and there was no adequate supply of replacements for planes lost in battle.

On the contrary, the losses of both the R.A.F. and the USAAF had declined as the ability of the Germans to attack had declined, and the forces were growing stronger every week.

Colonel Lawson told the crews at one briefing, "Flying for the Luftwaffe has lost much of its original glamor now that the balance of power has tilted heavily in favor of our Allied forces. All hope of air superiority for the Germans has gone. The fortress of Europe is crumbling in the east, while the Fifth and Eighth Armies are gnawing at the south."

Although the Westwall was as formidable as ever, the skies above it belonged to the Allies.

During May, it was obvious the numerous attacks on communications centers in France and Germany pointed toward an early date for the Allied troops to invade the Continent.

Group Commander Lawson briefed his staff. "Although the date for the invasion is top secret, it is apparent that it will be a great advantage to our troops to have the Germans working on supply lines in a constant state of disrepair.

"We will attack more in the role of a tactical force from now on."

"Does this mean we are abandoning strategic targets?" his operations officer said.

"Not at all. We shall continue to attack war factories, airfields, and marshalling yards."

In the British House of Commons, Prime Minister Winston Churchill declared, "The American Eighth Air Force has now exceeded the R.A.F. in size. With these immense forces at our disposal, our combined air forces will strike at countless targets in the immediate areas of France and the targets of western Germany."

It is impossible to give an accurate accounting of the bombing by both the British and the American Air Forces, but it is estimated that over one hundred fifteen thousand tons of bombs were dropped on various targets during the month. The average per day represented seven times the amount of bombs dropped on London by the German Air Force in one day.

On the eighteenth of the month, Colonel Lawson proudly read a commendation for the 365th Bombardment Squadron of the 305th. It cited the organization for sustained operations against Germany and her Allies by completing fifty-eight consecutive missions without loss.

"The 365th has consistently withstood opposition from antiaircraft defenses and the German Air Force by exemplary formation flying and courageous and effective defense spirit," Lawson read.

"The outstanding teamwork demonstrated by combat personnel has contributed immeasurably to attainment of this excellent operational record. The close support and continued efforts by personnel in all echelons of maintenance and administration has been invaluable."

It was signed by General Williams of the 1st Bombardment Division.

Group personnel felt keen pride in this accomplishment because the squadron had been one of the original units to blaze the trail for the Eighth Air Force in the early days.

General Williams also passed along a special commendation for the 422nd Squadron. It was issued by Supreme Headquarters, Allied Expeditionary Forces.

In lauding the officers and enlisted men of the unit for their vital contribution to the psychological preparation of the European Continent, it said, "The 422nd Bomb Squadron has been engaged in dropping leaflets for months, during which time they had dropped more than two hundred and fifty million leaflets over France, Belgium, Holland, Norway, and Germany. Reports from the continent indicate that we have been achieving many of our aims."

At month's end, culminating in the greatest aerial bombing in the history of the world, the power of the air blows rose toward the terrific climax of the invasion air support which was to be loosed within the week.

In this bombing, the 305th and the 1st Division played an outstanding role. They were justly proud of their record which, in the span of two years, had seen the bombing conception changed considerably, dwarfing those early missions that seemed so monumental at the time.

For months the intensity of the air attacks on Germany and Occupied Europe had grown to a terrific volume both by day and by night. The industrial targets of Germany had been hit hard. Now, for the past month, the coasts of France had been struck crippling blows.

The south of England was filled with troops of all

Allied nations waiting to invade Europe. The whole world was on edge for the invasion to start. And, on the sixth of June, the Allied armies landed on the beaches of France between Le Havre and the Normandy Peninsula to open the long-awaited western front against the Germans.

General Eisenhower told the invasion forces under his command, "If you see fighting aircraft over you, they will be ours."

This was no idle boast because Lieutenant General Werner Junck, commander of the German fighter defenses in the area, had only one hundred and sixty aircraft under his command and only eighty were operational. In the month following the invasion, the Reich could furnish him with only six hundred aircraft.

This gave the Allied Expeditionary Forces clear air superiority during the entire invasion operation.

In spite of increased activity for the 305th and the restriction on passes, morale had remained high during the exciting prelude to the invasion.

The crews appreciated the military necessity of maximum effort and were only too happy to take part in this momentous event.

On the eastern front, Russian troops were just outside the borders of the countries closest to Germany. In the south, the southern front was creeping up the boot of Italy daily, moving closer to the Brenner Pass and Germany.

The air war in June, as was expected, was stepped up to an almost unbelievable pitch with thousands of sorties flown nearly every day by all types of R.A.F. and American planes. There were everything from four-motored bombers to the smallest fighter over Europe almost every hour of the day.

Planes went out, not only once or twice, but even three times a day on occasion. The limit of endurance for crews and ground personnel alike was stretched to the breaking point so that troops on the coast of France would have adequate cover at all times, cover that amounted to complete domination of the skies over the beachheads.

In the 305th, the emphasis was on tactical targets for the three missions before the sixth of the month, but this was only a portent of things to come.

After D-Day, tactical objectives occupied the group for eight straight missions before a strategic target again was assigned to them.

German airfields in France, coastal defense installations, and communications targets kept turning up at briefings for eleven days after D-Day.

On the morning of June 6, the 422nd found itself in the briefing room receiving instructions for a daylight mission. This was something new and different for the crews. The leaflets were in French, for the consumption of civilians in important communications centers back of the landing zones.

They told the readers that their city would soon be subjected to intense aerial bombardment and urged them to leave the town quickly, avoid blocking the roads, and disperse in the country.

"You haven't a minute to lose!" they said. Since the air attacks began only one hour after the leaflets were dropped, this was no exaggeration.

The great French port of Cherbourg received constant attention from the 422nd. When the American lines had drawn up the Cherbourg Peninsula to the point where the battle for the city waged most fiercely, it was confronted with determined resistance by two German divisions.

At some cost to our forces, one of these was eliminated as an important factor in the defense. The other remained. A large-scale assault was prepared by the American troops and co-ordinated with it was a solo sortie by one of the 422nd planes, which dropped special leaflets urging the remaining defenders to surrender by pointing out their hopeless position.

Flying at fifteen thousand feet, flak gave Lieutenant England's crew grave concern. Not long after this, the American forces moved into the city itself.

The number of 422nd aircraft per mission rose during the month to ten or twelve from the customary five or six in the squadron. On several occasions, the targets were specifically requested by commanders of the ground forces in Normandy, and the number of prisoners taken in the first few days of fighting may be attributed in part to their work.

On the night of the thirteenth of June, the Germans put into use for the first time the installations they had built along the Pas de Calais by launching a series of pilotless aircraft and flying bombs which started dropping on London.

A steady stream of them continued night and day, keeping London under almost constant alert and causing considerable damage.

In the first days, the tendency was to scoff at this form of terror bombing by aircraft whose accuracy was erratic, but the serious side of the picture soon became evident in the face of real suffering by the people of London, who were subjected to this new form of attack.

Colonel Lawson assembled his group staff and told

them soberly, "We have been directed to divert our bombers from strategic targets to knock out the launching sites of these flying bombs."

There were protests from some of the group staff although they appreciated the desperate plight of the Londoners. Strategic planners always objected to any diversion of their forces for tactical operations.

Missions were set up in such haste that it was difficult for Colonel Lawson and his staff to determine the total amount of bombs used against the sites.

CHAPTER 14

Group Commander Lost in Action

COLONEL ERNEST LAWSON checked his notes before mounting the platform in the briefing room. The field order had come in only a few hours before, and now, at 1:25 A.M., the crews waited to hear what lay in store for them this eighteenth day of June.

They looked at him with respect. Many had known their group commander for months, and, after many trying periods together, they admired him both as a man and a combat flyer.

Lawson cleared his throat, and a hush descended over the thirty-one crews in front of him.

"We'll head a maximum force to attack oil refineries in Germany," he said. "I'll fly with the lead plane of the 40th Combat Wing piloted by Captain Claymore. There will be two formations, with Lieutenant Dressendorfer's crew at the head of the low group. Take-off time is 4:25 A.M."

The sincerity of his approach, completely lacking in bombastic oratory, suited their mood. They had a confident air, unmarred by vague apprehensions, a confidence gained through intelligent leadership at all levels of command.

"Pathfinder aircraft have been assigned to all forces," Lawson said, "in the event weather conditions prohibit visual bombing. Our particular target is an oil-refinery complex along the dock area at Hamburg.

"I'll be surprised," he said seriously, "if the Luftwaffe doesn't challenge our way to such a target." He paused momentarily, and his features lost some of their severity. "We won't be alone. Fourteen fighter groups will support our operations."

Scattered applause broke out but quieted when Lawson said, "All forces have been routed over the North Sea from separate points on the English coast."

Dressendorfer, heading the low group, turned to his copilot. "Pretty much according to plan. Only slight departures from the briefed route to the initial point."

Lieutenant Brye nodded. "We're a few minutes early, but that should be no problem."

Dressendorfer heard Lawson call for pathfinder bombing eight minutes before the IP. Flak reached the formations as they swept towards the target. Two minutes later, Dressendorfer snapped to attention. Over his head phones he heard. "Deputy, take the lead!"

"I wonder what happened?" he said to Brye anxiously.

"Flak must have struck home," the copilot said grimly. "It's been particularly intense around them."

Group Commander Lost in Action

They could see the wicked red flashes of fire around their own formation, with now and then a resounding boom echoing throughout their Fortress.

"Can you spot the target?" Dressendorfer called to the bombardier.

Lieutenant Redifer replied, "It's covered with a thin overcast, but the lead bombardier should have no difficulty.

"Bombs away!" he called.

The bombs plummeted earthward to join the tons of explosives heading for the oil refinery so far below them.

Dressendorfer, who had been watching the lead group closely, shuddered as Lawson's aircraft seemed to hang motionless in mid-air as a flak burst tore the tail off the Fortress.

"They'll never get out!" he said hoarsely. "It was a direct hit."

They watched with growing horror as the aircraft went into a flat spin and struck the ground with a flaming impact.

"Not a single chute," Brye whispered into the intercom.

They flew back without further incident, but the sudden disaster shocked even the most battle-hardened veterans. A pall of gloom descended on the 305th which took days to lift.

In spite of the loss, operations continued. A few days later, Colonel Anthony Q. Mustoe assumed command of the 305th.

After assembling the staff at the end of June, he discussed their operations in detail.

The Incredible 305th

"This month the group has rolled up a total of twenty-one day missions, seventeen leaflet operations, and twelve pathfinder missions," he said. "You can be proud of such a record."

He could see in their faces they were intensely proud of it, knowing full well what it had cost in sacrifices of men and planes.

Night operations had ended on June 25 when the crews of the 422nd were transferred to Cheddington. Leaflet operations would continue, but hereafter they would be the responsibility of the 858th Bombardment Squadron from that base.

Mustoe pursed his lips thoughtfully. "We've got a job to do in building the 422nd back to strength now that the night crews have gone," he said. "It is extremely important that the group operate at full strength for the important day missions ahead of us."

"Did we ever receive a report on the Hamburg raid?" Lieutenant Colonel MacDonald, group operations officer said.

"I was coming to that," Mustoe said. "We were thwarted repeatedly by bad weather in getting photographs following the raid." He picked up a pile of glossy photographs and passed them around. "As you can see, the refinery received extensive damage. Our losses were not in vain," he said soberly. "Right now fuel supplies for the Luftwaffe and the German ground forces are critical. We have contributed our part in making them so."

"How about the second Hamburg raid?" MacDonald said.

"Results of the strike on the twentieth were excellent. Many hits were scored on the refineries." He studied a photograph of that mission thoughtfully. "We can expect increasing mission emphasis aimed at Germany's fuel supplies. The mission of the twenty-fourth, when we bombed refineries making high-grade lubricants, is a typical case to point up the importance of such strikes to the whole Allied war effort," Mustoe said.

"Many of the missions we are running to Germany today no longer hold the terrors they once held for the early crews. Opposition has dwindled, and, on many missions, few fighters are encountered. Let me warn all of you," he said with an admonishing finger, "the crews must never relax their vigilance. Many men will still die in the skies over Europe before victory comes. Let's not have them die needlessly because of overconfidence. Keep reminding them at every briefing that the Germans are resourceful and talented fighters. They can still fight back, and they will have that capability for months to come!"

With the coming of July, the first excitement of the land campaign subsided, and the principal consideration of the Allied forces was the methodical build-up and expansion of the front.

Mustoe passed along the comments of General H. H. Arnold to members of the group when he congratulated all groups of the Eighth Air Force for their operations during June.

"The 305th, which has done its part in helping reduce Germany's oil output," Mustoe said at a briefing, "should appreciate General Arnold's comments when he says the success of the Allied landings in Normandy gives further eloquent testimony to the value of our operations."

. . .

The Incredible 305th

In the closing days of July, the power of Allied arms burst through the German lines with the first break-through in the sector facing the American troops south of Coutances.

After a bombardment by the greatest concentration of heavy bombers ever assembled on one target, American armored divisions broke through the German front and, within five days, were fighting in Brittany.

The 305th, and the other groups of the 1st Bombardment Division, received battle honors for participating in the Normandy campaign as well as battle honors for "Air Offensive, Europe."

There was such a sameness to the missions, despite their tremendous value to the war effort, that each day seemed but a continuation of the last. Missions were set up, briefed, and crews departed for the front. Gone were the days of spectacular air battles, although flak still struck violently at the formations reaching deeper and deeper into Germany.

Mustoe told them at one briefing, "It must be a sheer impossibility for the Germans to dispose of their limited fighter defenses against the massive forces of the USAAF and the R.A.F."

He paused a moment, deep in thought. "Our bombers now can strike deeply into Germany to blitz Munich, turn back on the next day to bomb the area immediately in front of Allied troops, or saturate Kiel in the night."

To add to the German's problems, Mustoe noted reports of sizable forces of heavy bombers in Italy consistently striking at the oil of Ploesti and the airplane factories of Austria, Hungary, and Rumania.

"It is incredible," Mustoe said with awe, "when you think of the magnitude of the Allied air forces. The Germans now have a complete lack of powerful aerial support which they used to couple with Panzer might to assure conquest. Today we can bring a greater number of planes to the aid of our ground forces at any given moment than the Germans ever could."

Air history was being made, and the 305th did its part in earning Lieutenant General Spaatz's commendation to the Eighth Air Force in which he cited several important factories, railroad stations, oil stores, and flying bomb installations as having been successfully attacked. From strategic missions to tactical, and back again, became the pattern of their daily activities.

During the last week of July, after the initial drive by the ground troops to Cherbourg had been completed, the progress of the troops in the beachhead slowed down considerably.

For the next two weeks, the front was stable until on the twenty-eighth General Bradley and General Patton struck into Brittany and on to Paris, turning the whole flank of the German Army to begin the complete rout of the Germans in France.

July had been a month of unseasonably bad weather so the total number of 305th attacks where visual bombing could be undertaken was smaller than the previous month.

Mustoe, in reading a report on the success of the twelve-plane formation, turned to MacDonald. "LeMay was right. He said a long time ago that the twelve-plane formation would contribute to the most accurate bombing."

"The eighteen-plane formation was perfect for the early days when we needed mass defensive power," the operations officer said.

Mustoe nodded assent. "The larger formation was only one stage of a continuing development of tactics in the Eighth."

"Do you have any precise figures in the report?" MacDonald said with interest.

"By all means. Since the twelve-plane formation came into use, it has shown a record of forty-six per cent of the bombs within one thousand yards of the aiming point." He looked up. "That's a six per cent increase!"

In August, the 1st Division regained its place in leading the Eighth Air Force in bombing accuracy which it had lost the previous month to the 3rd Division.

During the 305th's eighteen missions, they concentrated on enemy airfields, oil refineries, aircraft plants, fuel storage depots, and German ports.

Both Mustoe and MacDonald were concerned by the large turnover of combat personnel at this time, partially due to the loss of nineteen aircraft on operational missions. Of greater impact, however, was the re-assignment of a large number of combat personnel after completion of their tour of operations. The scale of the group's requirements was not reduced, but an influx of new crews from the States posed countless problems.

Field Marshal Montgomery expressed strong feelings of many high officers and officials who felt the European war would be over in November. "Such an historic march of events can seldom have taken place in history in such a short space of time," he said. Events seemed to justify this optimism.

At the end of the month, the Allies in France rapidly

Group Commander Lost in Action

advanced their front lines. Things happened fast. The "V-1" coast was liberated. Tactical air forces wreaked havoc on the fleeing, bumper-to-bumper Nazi convoys.

Missions of the 305th were correlated closely with the efforts of the ground forces as the First Army moved inside Germany.

Russia's westward advances, meanwhile, were cutting off the Southern Balkans aided by our Twelfth and Fifteenth Air Forces.

The 305th functioned particularly well in attacks prior to air-borne landings and the numerous strikes to attempt a paralysis of German communications despite bad weather which grounded their B-17's many days.

The experience level of key combat personnel was lowered again when the tour of combat for lead personnel was reduced to thirty missions. Over half of the lead crews automatically finished their tours by this reduction.

October began auspiciously for the Allied cause. American forces soon were east of the Siegfried Line north of Aachen and, by the tenth, the city was surrounded.

Marshalling yards, airfield installations, any target which could conceivably be destroyed to assist the ground forces, were attacked October 7. Three thousand heavy bombers were over Germany for a tremendous display of aerial might.

Hundreds of men in the 305th had been tirelessly performing these vital missions for months. Much of it was monotonous work yet it all became a part of the Allied victory in Europe.

Scores of men were lost in combat during this period, and, for the men who kept the planes flying, working late hours in mud, cold, and rain, it was a source of fierce pride that they finally were realizing the ultimate goal of mass daylight attacks by a co-ordinated bombing team of unmatched excellence.

For Colonel Mustoe, it had been an exhausting period but a rewarding one in which he shared with the group an immense satisfaction for their accomplishments.

Their feelings for him were readily apparent when he announced his transfer to command the 40th Combat Wing.

On everyone's lips, the refrain was the same. "The 305th's loss is the 40th's gain."

He had a few words to say before his departure.

"On relinquishing command of the 305th and this station, I wish to express my appreciation to all members of this command for the loyal support and generous co-operation you have given me.

"You have worked as a magnificent team and established an enviable record. I am confident you will not only uphold that record, but improve it and continue to be one of the finest fighting teams in the Air Forces.

"It has been a real pleasure to work with you, and I wish you good luck and good hunting."

They jumped to their feet impulsively. In a loud roar, they chanted, "The same to you colonel!"

Henry G. MacDonald moved up from the operations desk to replace him for the final climactic months of the war.

CHAPTER 15

The Underground

GAUNT AIRMEN, SOME almost caricatures of their former selves, began returning from prisoner of war camps as the advancing armies liberated them. Former veterans of the 305th found their old "Can Do" group had changed so much they hardly ever saw a familiar face.

They told gripping stories of escape and evasion that had the new members gaping with astonishment.

All crews had been indoctrinated in procedures to assist them in returning to friendly hands in the event of a bail out over enemy territory. Stark evidence of how agents in occupied countries had continually risked their lives to help fliers evade the Germans was vividly presented.

Lieutenant Neil H. Lathrop, a pilot of a B-17 from the 364th Squadron, told how he was shot down on a Ludwigshaven raid in January.

"After the target," he said, "the number three engine was knocked out by flak and could not be feathered and number one was running hot. The vibration forced me to leave formation, but we were already over France so I ordered the crew to jump."

Ten seconds later, he said, he changed his mind because he regained partial control of the aircraft.

"Keep your chutes on, I called the crew. We may be able to get back to England."

He described how they found cloud cover at fifteen hundred feet, but, when they broke into the clear, fighters jumped them.

Number two engine was riddled and started to smoke, he said. An explosion back of the cockpit set fire to the bomb bays. The elevator controls and the right aileron were hit.

"'Bail out!' I called as I hit the alarm bell. I checked each station to make sure no one had failed to hear the distress call. There was no answer."

His listeners hung on each word as he told how the elevator control cables snapped and the aircraft started to climb into a stall as he left his seat. "When I reached the hatch, I jumped while the aircraft was only nine hundred feet above the ground.

"I pulled the rip-cord immediately and saw a fighter circling the crew's chutes in the distance. I was still swinging when I hit the ground and winced as I hurt my back.

"Unhooking my parachute, I ran to a nearby farmer and shook hands.

"I said excitedly, 'Where are the Germans?'"

His listeners, intent on every word, learned how desperate his plight was when he said, "The farmer pointed

The Underground

in one direction so I ran in the opposite. I realized shortly that we had misunderstood one another. The farmer must have meant me to run the other way."

Lathrop's voice was full of emotion as he told about a small town which he hadn't seen at first hidden among the trees at the foot of a hill. "As I ran down the hill, I hastily discarded my flying equipment and burst out on a road and almost ran into a car surrounded by German officers. I did a quick about face and ran as hard as I could in the opposite direction."

He described how he thought, in slight panic, that they must have seen him. When shots sounded nearby, he jumped over some bushes and dove into the largest bush he could find.

His description was so realistic, they almost felt as if they were there with him as he said that, for three hours, armed Germans kept passing within a few feet while he held his breath.

"I noticed that the far side of my hiding place bordered on a well-beaten path. Once seven men stepped close enough to touch me, dropping a pile of the crew members' chutes and equipment while they argued with one another.

"I remained deathly still once when I thought a soldier was staring me in the eyes, but I was determined they would have to make me come out."

All eyes were fastened on his face as he described how, during the course of the search, the soldiers systematically poked staves through the bushes. "I was saved by two of the dumber ones who should have converged on my bush but instead stopped to talk."

There were quick intakes of breath from them as he continued. "After darkness I walked in the direction the farmer had pointed. It was sleeting now, and my back ached so I looked for a haystack. When this proved fruitless, I pulled some straw off a turnip shelter, but this inadequate cover prevented me from sleeping because of the chill air."

Deciding he might as well walk to keep warm, he told how he spotted a light in a stable, climbed a fence, and looked in.

"A boy was alone there so I opened the door. He was frightened half out of his wits. I told him not to be scared that I wouldn't hurt him.

"While I strode about the stable flapping my arms to restore circulation in my chilled body, I tried to express by sign language that I was thirsty.

"Although still frightened and bewildered, the boy brought me beer.

"When the boy went to bed, I crawled in beside him."

He described how he traded his leather jacket and one hundred francs for an old black coat with the boy. "It was coated with manure, but it came to my knees," he said with a chuckle. "Despite this, we both were pleased with the exchange."

Lathrop's fortitude and ingenuity were evident as he described how he took out his compass and escape map and decided to head for Paris. Although he had been warned that it was a dangerous city for an evader, he said, he reasoned that it would be easier to find help there.

They could appreciate his daring as he told how he jumped into ditches along the road whenever he heard traffic and how once when he turned a sharp corner he saw several German trucks parked with troops milling about them in the middle of the road.

"I knew I would look conspicuous if I turned back so I went right through them. To my surprise, I wasn't stopped. This reassured me because underneath my smelly coat I was wearing a green shirt and Army trousers."

He related that at the top of a hill, he saw a worker's camp along the road in the valley. The guards were just driving up. By the time he reached the vehicles, the soldiers were leaving them and falling into formation. "I elbowed my way through them without difficulty," Lathrop said.

"The first farm hand I approached could do nothing for me but supply tobacco. The second was too surprised to be of any help at all. I went on until I came to an isolated group of houses. In the backyard of the poorest house, an elderly man was chopping wood. He understood immediately and rushed me into the house."

Lathrop recounted that he was so starved that he grabbed the bread, butter, and wine which they eagerly gave him. The small piece of meat which he ate so quickly, he said, he learned later with regret, was their month's ration.

"I was given pants to wear over my Army trousers and a scarf to hide my shirt. In broken English, they told me the way to the nearest town, and I managed to get halfway through it without attracting attention."

He related how he stopped a young man in the middle of the town square and tried to tell him in pantomime who he was and that he needed help.

"I kept hearing words in French that sounded like, 'Comprends pas.'"

He told how he went on, thinking that the man took

him for a foreign worker, but he began to hurry when he saw the Frenchman approach the nearest German soldiers.

"When I left town, a German truck and trailer loaded with cement slowed down to go up hill. I was so tired of walking that I jumped into the back of the trailer where the driver and the armed guard couldn't see me. After riding for several miles, I realized the truck might turn into a camp when it was going too fast for me to jump off. The next time the truck slowed down for a grade, I leaped off and felt sharp pains jab at my injured back."

Walking became a painful task, he said, so when he saw another German truck loaded with bricks, he got on behind. He described how he waved in a friendly fashion as he passed people. What he didn't know, he said, was that the French would never hitch a ride on a German truck.

"A man on a bicycle asked me some questions which I could not answer. The Frenchman was so irritated that he quickly rode away."

He said he thought no more of the incident. Seeing a woman and a pretty young girl on the roadside, he jumped off the truck and approached the girl. She refused to have anything to do with him.

"The older woman knew some English and quickly learned that I was an American."

"'Are you hungry?'" she said.

"I nodded weakly so she took me to a farm house where I was fed.

"Later, my life was temporarily in danger because the Frenchman on the bicycle met me while I was being smuggled out of the country."

The Underground

"'German stool pigeon!'" the Frenchman roared.

"It was touch and go for my safety at first, but fortunately I had proof of my identity so I proceeded to England."

Events such as these were not uncommon, and thousands of men's lives were spared by courageous men and women in the occupied countries. They risked immediate death if they were caught, but this never deterred them. The brave fliers must be rescued and sent back to bomb again so their beloved countries once more would be free.

Another evader, Staff Sergeant William J. Koger, Jr., a tail gunner of the 422nd Squadron, was shot down in September, 1943, during an attack on Friedrichshafen.

"Over the target," he told interrogators, "I heard the pilot say we were running out of fuel. When we reached the German-French border on return, the number one engine was feathered in order to use less gas."

While intelligence officers took down his words in detail, he told how the B-17 traveled for another ten minutes when an FW-190 knocked out the number four engine in a sneak attack. They lost altitude, and it became necessary to leave the formation, he said.

"The P-47 escort came down to cover us," Koger said, "and they kept the 190's from doing any further damage."

He related how the escort was forced to leave them, however, as the fighters were low on gas themselves.

Fifteen FW's attacked them, he said, and their fuel transfer system was shot out.

"I heard the pilot say, 'We haven't enough gas to make the coast.'"

The tail gunner said that FW's, eight in line, came in

high at 6 o'clock. They flew to one hundred and fifty yards while the Fortresses' guns blazed away before breaking off the action.

He said he listened anxiously to the intercom, learning that the bombardier, radio operator, and the top turret gunner were wounded.

"The first two FW's of one wave made a pass at us. When a third followed them in, it exploded. The fourth kept coming and destroyed all interphone communications within the bomber."

With contact with the crew gone, he told the interrogators, he saw eight chutes below and decided the time had come to jump.

While the crippled B-17 lost altitude steadily he said, "I jumped at two thousand feet and pulled the rip-cord immediately. My shoes were jerked off when the chute opened, and, looking down, I saw our aircraft explode on the ground."

The intelligence officers were spellbound as he told how ground fire lashed at him as the Germans poured a hail of machine gun and rifle bullets towards him. "They missed me completely," he said, "but I counted eight holes through my parachute while I floated helplessly towards the ground."

He described how he landed hard in a wooded area on his back. He said he could barely move for ten minutes because his back was severely strained.

"Finally, I got to my feet and staggered off. Just then, a German soldier grabbed me by the arm. He could see that I was wounded.

"I was still dazed," Koger said, "but with all the strength I could muster, I swung at him. He hit the ground and lay there without making a sound so I started to run

The Underground

through the blackberry bushes."

After three hours, he said, he couldn't run another step, so he started to walk and continued until two o'clock the next day.

"I kept in the wooded area the whole time except twice when I had to cross highways. When this became necessary, I lay on the side of the road until I was sure it was clear and then made a wild dash."

In response to a question, he said there was no time to stop for food or drink. "I didn't even use my compass but put every ounce of strength into putting ground between me and the Germans. I learned later, when the German patrol reached him, the soldier I had struck was still unconscious."

He told how he lay under some trees, in his flying suit, and what was left of his stocking feet, when a boy spotted him.

"He just looked and ran to his house without speaking. Shortly, he was back with civilian clothes and I was helped to a house where my back was rubbed with liniment," he said gratefully. "They fed me and put me to bed. I didn't get out of that bed for four days."

He said the Germans searched systematically for him, so he had to hide in the woods again. He lay concealed on a hill top where he had a clear view of the German search.

"I remained there patiently, and, from time to time, the French managed to get food to me for which I was extremely grateful.

"The following day, I was taken from the hill and given a good supper. I learned to my amazement that these brave villagers had contacted the underground and soon I was on my way to safety."

CHAPTER 16

War of Attrition

NOVEMBER, 1944, WAS not a fateful month. It was a month in which the optimists had hoped peace would reign in Europe. It also was a month in which even the pessimists confessed that progress had been made towards that end.

"Wonder what ever happened to the sun?" was a common query as men cocked their heads on one side and squinted sourly at the low-hanging clouds.

No longer in the experimental stages, the pathfinder equipment was employed frequently and demonstrated that it was quite practical to run missions in the ugly weather.

The target was a familiar one on the second day of the month, but in this case familiarity had bred, not contempt, but a healthy respect for the defenses of I.G.

Farben-Industrie plant at Merseburg. Previous missions there had been as rough as any the crews had made.

Situated in the heart of a broad belt of flak batteries, it was more heavily defended than the German capital itself. Oil had become precious to the Germans as it became scarcer, and, as always when they rated a target highly important, the ground defenses were heavy.

Moreover, the area was well supplied with German air bases on which the unpredictable squadrons of the Luftwaffe could gather their dwindling strength for yet another attempt on the relentless bombers from across the Channel.

While the briefing officers studied the enemy capabilities, Colonel MacDonald told them, "The German Air Force has had a long rest, and this may be the day."

Events proved the accuracy of his foresight. The Luftwaffe came up in strength. They exacted a heavy toll in the greatest air battle the European skies had seen since bloody Schweinfurt more than a year before.

The Germans did not attack the twenty-four planes of the 305th, but German flak guns were trained accurately on the formations. Twenty-one B-17's suffered battle damage.

While the group's planes escaped fighter attacks themselves, evidences of enemy opposition were seen. Twelve FW-190's "ganged up" on a lone straggler. The P-51 escort immediately tackled them, but three of the enemy got through to the bomber.

A 305th airplane, returning alone with a feathered engine, saw four B-17's flying singly in the distance. The crew was shocked to see each of them catch fire under the savage pounding of the guns of the 190's.

An oil refinery near Hamburg succumbed in part to

the well-aimed bombs of the group two days later.

Oil refineries and marshalling yards needed constant attention, and the 305th did its part to destroy these vital installations.

Fortifications in the Metz area, held by the German forces opposed to General Patton's Third Army, were assigned to specially equipped aircraft, but visibility was so poor the group attacked a marshalling yard at Saarbrücken instead.

In such attacks, new methods were incorporated to indicate the "safety" line, the line beyond which planes could bomb without danger of hitting friendly troops. A regulated line of black bursts was sent up by friendly guns as one indicator. The other marker was an indicator which, by changing color on the instrument panel, showed that the bombers were in the clear. The crews approved of this, but they were not so sure of the flak line.

Synthetic oil refineries and tactical targets consumed the balance of the month for a total of twelve missions.

When Colonel MacDonald studied the results, one thing was clear. "Enemy defenses retain considerable effectiveness," he told the crews. "Although fighter opposition was non-existent for us, the Luftwaffe made some of its strongest efforts in more than a year against other groups. Flak remains a potent killer," he warned.

Merseburg, in particular, now was regarded by the crews as Berlin once was.

By December, the power of the American, British, and later the French armies pushed the Germans back across France, Belgium, and part of Holland. This had happened in a series of lightning sweeps, but, as the borders of Germany were reached, a longer war of attrition began.

The Incredible 305th

Behind the lines, the vast problem of building up supplies for the next push went on. All along the line both the Allies and the Germans probed continually for weak spots in one another's defenses.

Winter played into the hands of the Germans on all fronts, holding down the bombers by fog over the bases, and hiding the targets in clouds when the bases were clear in England.

For the 305th, weather made instrument attacks necessary on all but two of their thirteen missions.

While the unexpected German offensive of December sixteenth rolled through the lines in the Ardennes sector, the group felt frustrated. During the period between the thirteenth and twenty-third of December, their forces, which could have helped to stem the tide, were grounded due to unfavorable weather.

When it was possible to fly again, two visual missions were carried out on German airfields and communications centers. For the balance of the month, the emphasis continued on tactical targets—targets which had a direct bearing on the critical support for Germany's armies.

Colonel MacDonald discussed the month with his staff on New Year's Eve.

"Do you realize," he said, "that we have completed a whole month of operations without once encountering the German Air Force?"

His tones of incredulity were reflected in each of their worn faces.

"We've been lucky," his intelligence officer said. "Other groups have not been so fortunate. During the latter half of the month, the Luftwaffe rose to challenge many of the other bomber formations."

"I'm sure the crews are fed up with my harping on the subject," the wiry colonel said. His square face showed the strain of months under constant pressure. "But men will still die in the skies over Germany before we've seen the end of the war. I don't want any of them to lose their lives foolishly. Only after the last Nazi fighter has risen to the attack, and the last gun has been fired into the skies, can we relax our vigilance."

CHAPTER 17

Massive Aerial Assault

WITH THE OPENING of the new year, the bombing offensive against Germany was resumed. Along the whole western front there was a growing need of support for the ground troops, especially in the Ardennes sector, where the supply of the American First and Ninth Armies was disrupted and losses continued to rise.

On New Year's Day, the Luftwaffe took the offensive with effects that spelled disaster for its dwindling power.

This was just another day of work for the 305th whose only concession to the occasion was an increase in the number of planes dispatched to forty-five instead of the usual thirty-six.

The lead squadron bombed Gettingen, unloading its bombs on the eastern side of the marshalling yards when the undercast blocked the aiming point. The other two squadrons also bombed yards.

Meanwhile, nine planes of the group joined planes of the 92nd Group to form a screening force. They ran into serious trouble when they encountered fifteen FW-190's which caught them at a moment when their fighter escort was not around.

The German fighters launched a series of attacks which continued for eight minutes.

The besieged Forts fought back fiercely, but six B-17's, including four from the 305th, went down.

Their worst enemy, the coldest January since 1890, brought the most sustained cold spell they had experienced. The first two winters in England had been mild by comparison, and snow had fallen only in quickly disappearing flurries.

Frost silvered the branches of the trees and clung precariously to the forgotten barbed wire, which still stood in the fields ready to repel the attack of an enemy who had long since given up hope of "sailing for England." And there was real snow that stayed on the ground for days, on end, and came again to harass the men on snow detail.

Tactical missions, including a bridge over the Rhine, were requested by the ground forces. This target was typical of the ones the group attacked during the month because they were critical points in the German transportation system.

February was the last month when the German Armies on the continent could be reckoned as a formidably organized army.

During the month, the advantages gained by the sudden push of the Germans through the Ardennes sector were erased. Once more the initiative moved back into the hands of the Allied commanders and the rout of the German western army began.

In the air, the war went on much as it had been moving for the past year. Day after day fleets of planes were over Germany, chopping the rail and communications lines to pieces behind the German Armies and striking strategic blows at the industries of the Reich.

It was the most merciless air offensive man had ever conceived as it pounded targets day and night. There was little need now to bomb the countries occupied by the Reich. The target was Germany.

From the Ruhr to Berlin in the north, from Saarbrücken to Vienna in the south, a city or town of Germany was devastated every day.

If the Eighth was grounded, the Ninth Air Force was out. If the day saw little activity, the night was filled with the sound of the Royal Air Force off to stoke the fires of destruction throughout the heart of Germany.

Among the sixteen missions the group flew during February were a pair of attacks on Berlin. They were the heaviest assaults in the tortured life of the German capital.

Despite the fact the Luftwaffe tried to stretch its tired wings to defend "Big B," no enemy air opposition materialized against the 305th's planes.

Enemy flak gunners were by no means so co-operative. Their fire was only moderate, but it was accurate enough to score hits on every plane in the lead and high squadrons.

One flak burst hit the nose of the lead aircraft of the high squadron. Lieutenant G.F. French, in the bombardier's compartment, was knocked away from his sight, his oxygen supply was cut, and glass from the shattered nose blew in his face. Nevertheless, he recovered sufficiently to release his bombs on the target.

Over the German radio came confused wailings about the tragic fate of the German nation, crying that this had been the hardest blow Berliners had been called on to endure. The whole center of the city had been dealt a staggering blow, more than London ever had been called on to endure.

The surge of activity at the end of the month had kept the 305th busy from day to day handling the missions. It did not end with the twenty-eighth of February, as the early days of March were to demonstrate.

The second day of March, the 305th had flown its 300th daylight mission. The many night missions flown by the 422nd Squadron, and a few other miscellaneous chores, were not counted in this total.

With the field-order assignment of groups for the mission that day came word that the 305th would lead the First Air Division.

"This is a tough assignment," lanky Lieutenant Colonel Howell G. Crank told the crews. "Groups following the 305th into the flak-thick Leipzig area are to bomb the Bohlen and Rositz oil plants. The 305th, being first in, has been given a concentration of flak guns at the target."

Since it was a division lead, the deputy group leader was assigned as air commander.

With him at the head of the bomber column was an all-star crew which included men on their second tours. They were Major Robertson, group navigator, who also had flown with the R.A.F., and Captain Flanagan, group PFF navigator. Captain Ten Eyck was the pilot, and the squadron bombardier and navigator of the 365th were in the plane.

The first crews to return for interrogation reported the loss of the plane. Each succeeding crew told its story in a way that showed how strong an impression the event had made on them.

It was a tough blow to take so late in the war. Colonel Crank, with his level-headed, down-to-earth outlook and an easy-going sense of humor, was well liked by the combat men.

Events were moving at such a furious pace that Colonel MacDonald wished there were more than twenty-four hours in a day and seven days in a week to accomplish the enormous scope of the action. There were so many targets to be bombed in support of the ground troops.

The campaign, which started in the latter part of February, dragged into March, but it didn't drag very much.

All along the western front the Allies were stirring, moving forward slowly, edging in around Cologne, thrusting north and south of that great city on the Rhine, and with tremendous power backing the cautious scouting parties prodding the German armor at different points.

The Air Forces were there, too, and throughout the month the pace of the bombing was stupendous. Every possible line of communication open to a German unit in the west was blitzed by the Eighth Air Force and the tactical air forces on the Continent.

Colonel MacDonald wisely put another word of warning into all the good news coming from the battle fronts.

"I don't think there is any need to tell you about the

news, nor the effect it should have on your work. A month or six weeks may see this thing through, and now is a poor time to let down."

The weather was kind to the 305th during the month, and a rapid succession of missions were flown to prepare the way for the growing offensive of the ground troops, which reached a climax when they crossed the Rhine.

Many of the missions were visual, and the 305th's bombardiers rose nobly to the occasion. Strike pictures presented irrefutable evidence of devastating accuracy.

The crushing weight of the Allied air offensive reached its heaviest point of the war in March when the Eighth Air Force dropped seventy-three thousand tons of bombs on the Reich.

After the middle of March, the Allied armies surged across the Rhine, sweeping the once invincible Wehrmacht before it.

While the 305th worked, they could feel the promise of ultimate success growing stronger. The reports of the progress of the armies, and the very tenor of the work they performed in sending bombers to their vital targets, combined to form a conviction that the end was drawing near.

Churchill said, "This is the last great heave."

Montgomery called it, "The last round."

The GI, who was less inclined to find a striking phrase for the work he was doing, understood what they meant and fought on.

They all had a more confident feeling than the feverish excitement that followed the race across France. This time, everyone realized the war was not going to end in a miraculously quick decision.

Rumors were rampant, keeping pace with the headlines in the newspapers. Old ones were revived, dusted off, and freshened up for the current situation. Even one or two new ones made their debut.

"We're going off operations on April 15," a sergeant said.

"You know," a friend said, "I heard the same thing about August 15, 1944."

A pilot whispered to his navigator during a briefing, "British appraisers are looking over the field. They're getting ready to take over again."

"Is that right?" the navigator said. "You know, I heard an R.A.F. sergeant in Rushden say his outfit was all set to move in here. It must be true."

When Colonel MacDonald was told about this particular rumor, he said with a chuckle, "That R.A.F. sergeant is a patient character. He's been 'all set to move in for years now.'"

There was less disposition to believe the rumors toward the end of the month. Yes, they were eager to hear a good rumor because rumors added spice to routine.

The kidding type of rumor was cropping up, a parody on the latrine-o-grams that had swept the base so often before.

"You know that new landing in the Philippines?" a lieutenant would say.

"Yeah..."

"Well, one of the initial outfits they sent ashore was a bunch of Seabees. The first thing they did was put up a big sign with 'Welcome, 305th' on it!"

April ushered in one of the most exciting months in the history of mankind.

Thousands upon thousands of Allied airplanes were out daily shooting up roads, bridges, rail lines, cars, locomotives, boats, and airplanes. With no fuel to fly them, enemy planes sat helplessly on the ground and became easy victims to the relentless attackers. By the hundreds they were destroyed daily until the climax of destruction was reached during the month when more enemy planes were destroyed in one day than there were heavy bombers in the First Air Division.

From a certainty at the beginning of the month that the war in Europe soon would be over, Allied enthusiasm rose to fever pitch by the end of the month as unconditional surrender rumors spread thick and fast.

Unbelievable advances were made daily as chaos grew within the Reich and the Wehrmacht. Heavy bomber missions were scrubbed just before take-off, or even recalled when part way to the target, after it was found the target had just been captured by a flying tank column.

In the last month of offensive operations in Europe for the group, they experienced intense activity during the first half by flying fifteen missions in the first nineteen days.

Most of them were sledge-hammer blows against enemy communications and disappearing air power.

When the strain of the almost daily missions relaxed after the nineteenth day of April, the base was able to turn its attention to a more intensive study of what the ground troops were up to.

"The end of the war is drawing constantly closer," MacDonald told the group. "It is apparent that, except for the possibility of the Germans establishing one more defense line on the Elbe, the key to victory in Europe is turning."

The total absence of enemy opposition on many of April's missions was another indication of Germany's

Massive Aerial Assault

plight. Among the flying personnel, a healthy respect persisted until the end for the enemy's flak batteries.

With the Russians fighting in Berlin and the Ninth Army on the Elbe, the end was close.

After several missionless days, the 305th took off on its last offensive operation in the European war on the twenty-fifth of April. The target was the famed Skoda munitions plant at Pilsen, Czechoslovakia. The seven-tenths cloud cover made sighting difficult, and two of the squadrons had to make three runs before releasing their bombs.

The low squadron's bombardier got a break in the clouds finally, and, working fast, he was able to put the bombs squarely on the aiming point.

The high squadron, given visual conditions at the last minute after starting a pathfinder run, strung its bombs across the plant area.

There was no sign of the Luftwaffe, but the flak knocked two ships out of formation, one of which later returned to base. The gunners on the ground seemed to grow more proficient with each run, and they achieved very accurate fire on the third runs.

For the rest of April, the group flew no missions.

Their upturned faces reflected their pride as MacDonald stood before them in the briefing room. "And finally I can say truthfully," he said, "the trip to Pilsen is the last job of the war for the 305th."

It was the 337th daylight bombing operation the "Can Do" group carried out. It also was a fitting climax to the long and brilliant record of the 305th's veterans.

CHAPTER 18

Symbol of Triumph

AFTER TWO AND a half years of aerial combat in Europe, the month of May, 1945, passed without a single mission flown by the 305th Group. The constant strain of missions lifted, and the comparative inactivity required a mental readjustment for all the men at Station 105.

These men had pioneered the philosophy of daylight, precision bombing of strategic targets. Their record established beyond all doubt the incontrovertible fact that nowhere were the enemy's war plants safe from visual aerial attack.

They had helped to prove that day bombing permitted destruction of relatively small targets. They proved that a compact force could destroy individual plants because of greater bombing accuracy.

Despite criticism and disappointments, their accomplishments were a testament to the vision, skill, and courage of airmen like LeMay who worked out the techniques. He was one of a few who foresaw the employment of large-scale aerial might. In defiance of great physical obstacles and bitter enemy resistance, such men finally proved their points.

The Air Force dropped seven hundred and one thousand, three hundred tons of bombs on enemy targets in Europe, including five hundred and thirty-one thousand, seven hundred and seventy-one tons on targets in Germany itself. There were four million, three hundred and seventy-seven thousand, nine hundred and eighty-four high explosives used, and more than twenty-seven million small incendiaries.

The Eighth destroyed fifteen thousand, four hundred and thirty-nine enemy aircraft in its furious campaign of attrition against the Luftwaffe, more than all other American air forces in Europe and Africa combined. Fighters of the Eighth shot down five thousand, two hundred and thirty-one enemy planes in the air, and destroyed four thousand, two hundred and seven on the ground by strafing.

Gunners on the bombers shot down six thousand and one. These figures did not include the undetermined thousands of German aircraft destroyed or damaged on the ground by bombing.

On all types of operations, six hundred and sixteen thousand aircraft were dispatched. Of these, three hundred and thirty-two thousand, six hundred and forty-five were heavy bombers. Supply lines were taxed heavily just to supply the more than one billion gallons of fuel which were consumed.

During the last year of the war in Europe, the Eighth

Symbol of Triumph

dispatched an average of twelve hundred aircraft every day.

While their accomplishments hastened the end of the war immeasurably, they necessarily took their terrible toll in human life. Casualties in the Eighth were forty-three thousand, seven hundred and forty-two airmen killed or missing in action, and one thousand, nine hundred and twenty-three seriously wounded.

The 305th lost one hundred and seventeen airplanes during the war and six hundred and sixty-five men were killed in action.

Through the years, over seven thousand men had been assigned to the group.

Gunners claimed a total of three hundred and fourteen enemy aircraft during the five hundred and forty-five missions flown by the group.

Countless tens of thousands of American, British, and Russian lives were saved as a result of their operations. Attacks prevented submarines from sailing, planes from taking off, and locomotives and trucks from having the fuel to haul supplies and ammunition for use against Allied troops.

The Eighth had demonstrated very early what had been doubted in Europe that daylight precision bombing could be done without prohibitive losses. The losses often were high, but the courage and tenacity of men like those in the 305th carried them through.

The success of the concept behind the Eighth was learned fully only after the invasion of Germany. The relatively light casualties of the Allied Expeditionary Forces, the shattered factories, the statements of German industrialists and military leaders, these told the story of what the Eighth had accomplished in the war against Germany.

At a special ceremony at 1st Air Division Headquarters on May 4, some former members of the 305th were decorated with the Croix de guerre by a French Air Force General.

Selected for the honor on the basis of their contributions to the liberation of France while serving with the group were Colonel Mustoe, Colonel Sault, Major Webb, and Major Singer, all of whom were now serving with the 40th Combat Wing.

While they were congratulated in French by the dignified representatives of France's air arm, other 305th officers were similarly honored in absentia, including Colonel MacDonald who was away at the time.

They learned also they had been awarded four more battle honors including those for Northern France, Ardennes-Alsace, Central Europe, and the Rhineland.

With ten or fifteen eager groundlings in each aircraft, B-17's roared off the runways and set course for the Ruhr on almost daily flights. The missions were far different now. Instead of bombs, they carried sight-seers. Instead of bombing, the object was rubber-necking.

In a large-scale program to show the ground personnel of the group the damage done by the planes they put in the air, formations carried approximately two thousand delighted "paddlefeet" over the shattered cities of the Ruhr and Rhineland.

The seven-hour ride left the passengers tremendously impressed with the effectiveness of bombing and the Allied war machine. The crumpled Siegfried Line, the devastation at Aachen, the bleak rubble of the Ruhr industrial centers, the numerous bomb-pocked airfields,

Symbol of Triumph

and the gigantic prison camp on the Rhine produced a lasting impression of Allied might and air power on the observers. If any further proof was needed, this definitely established the fact that their efforts had been worthwhile.

Nobody was surprised when May 8 was declared V-E Day. While everyone was aware the announcement would almost inevitably prove to be an anticlimax, the complete absence of any triumphal celebration nevertheless came as a particularly abrupt letdown.

For weeks the newspapers had been proclaiming vociferously that the "last hours" were at hand, and that it was "all over but...." By May 7, it was perfectly clear that the war was formally ended, but still the announcement was withheld.

On the morning of May 8, the station's complement assembled in the main hangar at nine o'clock. Lieutenant Colonel Graybeal, substituting for MacDonald, briefly reviewed the group's achievements and gave them permission to "take off" until Thursday to celebrate.

Chaplain Morkowski said a prayer of thanksgiving and recalled the final sacrifice made by many men of the group. The band played the national anthem, and the assemblage dispersed.

There was no demonstration, except by a few eager individuals who made for their quarters at top speed to prepare for their pass.

It was a strange scene. The men returned from the hangar in small groups of two and three, walking unconcernedly along the tarred roads and talking quietly among themselves. They had just helped to win a war, but there was little in their outward appearances or conversation to reveal the fact. They looked more as if they were simply returning from the first show at the base theater.

Two hours later, a teletype message brought word that all Eighth Air Force installations were to be restricted for V-E Day. Any last vestige of high spirits was erased by that announcement.

Along with several other groups, the 305th shared in a "revival" operation during the month, flying to Eastern Germany to pick up liberated American prisoners.

At least half a dozen former 305th combat men found themselves riding once again in the green-striped B-17's, and reunions among old friends were common.

A fitting climax in recognition of the group's efforts occurred when Colonel MacDonald returned from headquarters on the continent with a huge Nazi flag, fifteen feet long and eight feet wide.

When all personnel of the station assembled in hangar two, they stared popeyed at the blood-red Nazi banner displayed over the platform.

MacDonald mounted the steps to explain. "This flag was flying over the city of Schweinfurt when the 42nd 'Rainbow' Division captured the German ball-bearing center with only sixty casualties."

They stood ramrod stiff as the colonel addressed them. They recalled vividly this greatest of all battles of the air when their heavies fought their way through fighter-filled skies to bomb the vital plants.

Typifying the sacrifices made by the Air Force to knock out the enemy industry, the 305th lost thirteen out of the fifteen Flying Fortresses it sent on the October 14 mission.

MacDonald told how the Army commander had remembered the Eighth's sacrifices and realized that their destruction of the strategic bombing targets was directly connected with the feeble opposition the Wehrmacht presented.

"Major General Collins, commander of the 42nd," the colonel said, "decided the captured Nazi emblem would be a fitting symbol of triumph for the Eighth's air warriors. Accordingly, he sent the flag to General Spaatz.

"He selected the 305th because our operations were typical of the Eighth's performance on the crucial Schweinfurt missions.

"I'm sure you all join me," MacDonald said, "in thanking the Rainbow Division for this trophy which is the first of its kind to be given to an air force unit in this theatre."

The colonel pointed to a corner of the flag. "The inscription reads, 'To the Eighth Air Force. The Rainbow has revenged your losses at Schweinfurt!'"

Strong and sturdy men, who had never shown emotion in combat, found unaccustomed tears trickling down their cheeks, and, for those with more intimate memories, the tears came unashamedly in a flood.

EPILOGUE

At the end of hostilities in Europe, the 305th was assigned the task of mapping the Continent, including parts of North Africa, Iceland, and Greenland.

The entire unit was converted into a photomapping outfit. Although not trained for this highly specialized work originally, the group performed the assignment in a most efficient manner.

The 305th then was de-activated in Europe and members of the proud organization either returned to civilian life or joined other organizations in the Air Force.

The uneasy peace following World War II ended in 1950 when the Communists invaded South Korea and the world again was faced with the dread of total war.

Localization of that conflict can be credited primarily to the magnificent fighting spirit of America's ground troops and a superbly trained organization known as the

Strategic Air Command whose jet bombers and atomic weapons gave the Russians pause in their grandiose schemes of world domination.

Curtis E. LeMay, commander of SAC, and now a three-star general, had fought long and tirelessly for strong, strategic air power to deter the aggressive intentions of any future enemy.

The Russians knew that if they started World War III, they would be engulfed in atomic fire. It was an appalling prospect, and they fought a delaying action of limited aid to the Chinese and North Koreans without throwing the full weight of their own armed forces into the conflict.

Headquarters, United States Air Force, authorized the activation of additional units to meet this new challenge. When SAC's deputy commander got the go-ahead, he thought it prudent to consult LeMay because he might have some ideas of his own as to which organizations should be re-activated.

"General," he said, "we now have formal authorization to increase the strength of the command."

LeMay nodded his head in agreement but remained non-comittal.

"After consultation with the staff, I have prepared a list of former groups which can be re-activated under our new wing concept."

He handed the list to LeMay who, without glancing at it, dropped it on his desk.

There was a long pause while the deputy shuffled uneasily in front of his commander's desk. He coughed nervously a couple of times, but LeMay seemed lost in a dream world, and his eyes had a faraway look that was most disconcerting.

"General LeMay," he said cautiously, "don't you have any personal choices?"

LeMay slowly leaned forward, and his eyes became animated as if some inner fire was forcing itself to the surface.

"Sir, the list...!"

"I hear you!" LeMay snapped.

"But, sir," he said with astonishment mounting in him, "don't you have even one recommendation?"

LeMay controlled himself with an effort. He said softly, "I don't care which groups you re-activate."

His deputy's mouth dropped open in disbelief, and he was about to protest when LeMay interrupted him. "I don't care which ones," he said with a voice quivering with emotion, "just so long as the 305th is *first!*"

A delighted smile broke across the face of the deputy, but only a flickering smile of satisfaction appeared on LeMay's face before it was reset in the familiar stern lines.

NAM. BRAVO COMPANY.

THE EXPLOSIVE NEW FILM— AND NOW, THE SEARING NEW NOVEL!

PLATOON
a novel by Dale A. Dye
based on a screenplay by Oliver Stone

0-441-67069-5 $3.50

Available at your local bookstore or return this form to:

CHARTER
THE BERKLEY PUBLISHING GROUP, Dept. B
390 Murray Hill Parkway, East Rutherford, NJ 07073

Please send me the titles checked above. I enclose _____. Include $1.00 for postage and handling if one book is ordered; add 25¢ per book for two or more not to exceed $1.75. CA, IL, NJ, NY, PA, and TN residents please add sales tax. Prices subject to change without notice and may be higher in Canada. Do not send cash.

NAME _____
ADDRESS _____
CITY _____ STATE/ZIP _____

(Allow six weeks for delivery.)   C6A